Adventure on
Dolphin Island

Adventure on
Dolphin Island

Ellen Prager

Illustrations by Kalon Baquero

iUniverse, Inc.
New York Lincoln Shanghai

Adventure on Dolphin Island

iUniverse books may be ordered through booksellers or by contacting:

iUniverse
2021 Pine Lake Road, Suite 100
Lincoln, NE 68512
www.iuniverse.com
1-800-Authors (1-800-288-4677)

ISBN-13: 978-0-595-35791-8 (pbk)
ISBN-13: 978-0-595-80260-9 (ebk)
ISBN-10: 0-595-35791-1 (pbk)
ISBN-10: 0-595-80260-5 (ebk)

Printed in the United States of America

For the curious, the adventurous, and all who care about the sea.

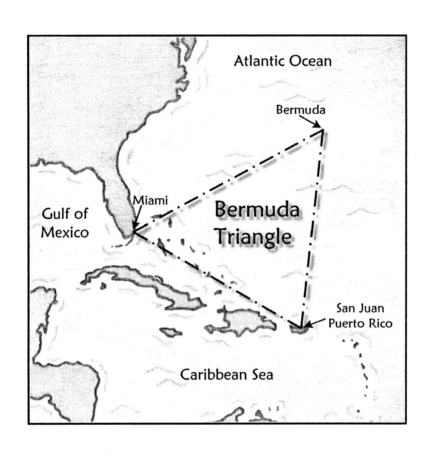

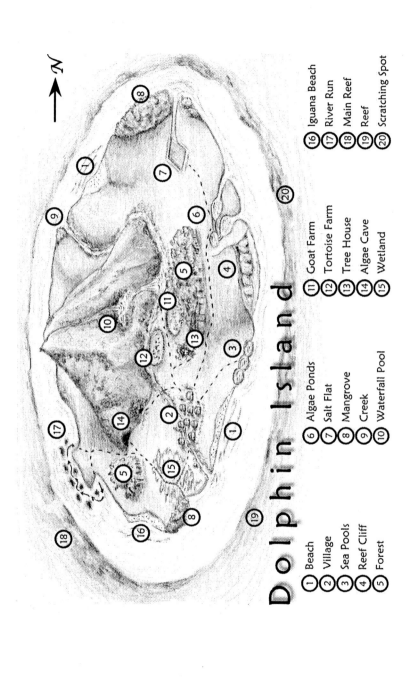

Dolphin Island

1. Beach
2. Village
3. Sea Pools
4. Reef Cliff
5. Forest
6. Algae Ponds
7. Salt Flat
8. Mangrove
9. Creek
10. Waterfall Pool
11. Goat Farm
12. Tortoise Farm
13. Tree House
14. Algae Cave
15. Wetland
16. Iguana Beach
17. River Run
18. Main Reef
19. Reef
20. Scratching Spot

1

It seemed like just minutes and the storm was upon them; it was moving incredibly fast. Never before had young Kelly or anyone in her family seen a sky so black. Low, dark clouds were rolling toward them as if carried on the breath of a giant. It looked as though they would soon engulf the top of the sailboat's mast. As the ominous mist got closer, the wind blew stronger and stronger. Waves were now coming from all directions and they were growing in size. Large raindrops began to fall.

Twelve-year-old Kelly Wickmer looked over at her father; he kept glancing her way, and as the wind strengthened, the concern on his face grew. She had spent the first two weeks of their sailing trip miserably seasick. With each wave her stomach had done flip-flops; she had stumbled around the deck and had refused to swim in what she was sure were shark-infested waters. On the boat and at sea, she was like a fish out of water. Of course, her older brother, fifteen-year-old Thomas, had taken to sailing and snorkeling as if he'd been born to it. Like in everything else, he was the adventurous, confident one. Thomas always did everything better than Kelly.

Her father had said the purpose of the month-long voyage aboard the rented sailboat was to allow them to spend time together as a family, but Kelly knew he had arranged the trip also hoping that she would get over her fear of the sea and gain some self-confidence. Well, it wasn't working and the approaching storm was definitely making things worse.

"Looks like we've got a blow—probably just another squall that'll push through quickly," observed Kelly's father, James Wickmer, as he put on his rain gear.

"Honey," he added to his wife, Caroline, "you and Thomas get on your foul weather gear to help take down sail and secure lines. We'll have to steer the boat by hand. The autopilot's been acting a little too squirrelly for this kind of weather. Kelly, you go down below, sit tight, and listen to the radio for the next weather report."

"It's nothing to worry about," reassured Kelly's mother. "This is a very safe boat and your dad's a great sailor. It'll be bouncy for just a little while."

"I'm going to start the engine," shouted Mr. Wickmer over the strengthening wind. "Thomas, take the helm while your mother and I go forward to haul in the sails. Make sure we stay headed into the waves."

"Aye, aye, captain," replied Thomas excitedly, putting on his rain jacket. As he passed by Kelly he whispered, "Yeah, you just stay down below where it's safe, baby, while we do the work up top."

Thomas was constantly tormenting his shy younger sister. His athletic good looks and personality made him enormously popular at school and, in fact, everywhere they went. Kelly always felt in the shadow of her older brother and rather average in general. Her straight, dark-blond hair was average looking; she was average in height, in school, and in sports. No one ever seemed to notice her at all. She was particularly jealous of her brother's confidence, and his teasing made her feel even worse about herself.

With the rest of her family up on deck, Kelly went down below. She looked around. Oh, how she hated the wretched sailboat with its narrow bunks and tiny kitchen, to say nothing of the toilet that swayed from side to side when she tried to use it or the shower that was the size of a coffin. She desperately missed her friends, her favorite television shows, and her computer. She wanted nothing more than to be back home in Massachusetts and on dry land. And now, she was down below, by herself, as the boat pitched wildly in the developing storm.

All alone, Kelly's fear was escalating. She was on the verge of panic. She didn't want to stay below, all by herself. Thinking that it would be better to be up on deck with the rest of her family, she put on her rain gear, climbed up the short ladder, and went through the hatchway.

Once on deck, the wind and rain pelted Kelly's face. It felt like needles hitting her skin. As the boat rolled beneath her feet, she fell onto one of the benches in the cockpit, grabbing for something to hold onto. In front of her, Thomas was at the helm fighting to keep the wheel in the right position and the sailboat headed into the waves. Her mother and father were up at the front of the boat working on the sails. Not the front, she remembered—it was called the bow in sailing lingo. Her brother made fun of her when she didn't use the right nautical terms.

She looked out across the dark, rain-swept sea. Waves that had been small rolling hills just an hour ago were now towering mountains. The ship pitched up and down as it rode over and through the monstrous walls of water. When a wave struck at an angle, the sailboat rocked violently from side to side. Kelly gripped the side of the boat, wishing she were somewhere else, anywhere else.

Her brother was now yelling at her, but the noise from the strong wind was too loud. She couldn't hear what he was saying. Then she noticed, a little too late, that in addition to his foul weather gear her brother had put on a harness with a line that clipped onto the ship's railing.

Suddenly, a huge wave crashed into the sailboat and a powerful surge of water washed over the deck. Thomas and her parents were knocked off their feet, but their harnesses kept them aboard. Kelly was not so lucky. In an instant she was swept off the deck and into the angry ocean.

Kelly's parents quickly scrambled back to the helm to make sure that Thomas was all right and that the boat was still heading into the oncoming waves. If the ship went broadside and one of the huge waves hit it squarely on the side, the sailboat could flip. With the wind howling and the rain slashing down, they couldn't hear what Thomas was shouting—though they did notice that he was pointing to a missing life buoy and gesturing wildly about something going overboard.

Thomas pointed to the open hatchway that led below and yelled at the top of his lungs, "*KELLY!*"

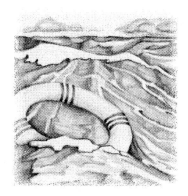

2

It had happened so quickly. Kelly didn't know where she was or exactly how she had gotten there. But somehow, she was now underwater surrounded by swirling foam and bubbles. All she knew was that she needed air and she needed it quickly. But where was the surface? Which way was up? Then she remembered that when she looked up from the bottom of the deep end in the pool, the surface always looked brighter. Kelly focused on where the water was the lightest and kicked as hard as she could, pulling in wide strokes.

Breaking through to the ocean's surface, she gasped for air, sucking in giant breaths. Frantically, she looked around. Where was the boat? All she saw was water and all she heard was the howling of the wind.

The sea was like a washing machine of wind and water—and Kelly was in the middle of the spin cycle. She spit out seawater and screamed for help, trying to keep her head above the surface. Where was the boat? Did her parents know that she had fallen overboard? Did Thomas see her go, and would he even say anything if he did? Kelly was sure that any minute she would see the sailboat and her parents would come back to get her. But the minutes dragged on and nothing appeared. She focused on keeping her head up so that she could breathe in air, not seawater. Soon her legs began to tire from treading water. Her head ached and she started to cry, thinking back to when her dad had first proposed the idea of taking a month-long sailing trip.

For her brother, the idea of a sailing trip was just the adventure he had been waiting for. After all, his favorite movie was *Pirates of the Caribbean* and he was obsessed with the television show *Survivor.* For Kelly, it had sounded like her worst nightmare. She had dreaded the thought of being trapped on a boat with her brother and parents for a month, with nothing to do but look out at an endless sea of water. And while she loved to swim in a pool, she was terrified of the ocean. All those shows on the Discovery Channel showed sharks attacking people and bloody wounds. She had also read about jellyfish, stingrays, and other scary things that lived in the sea. In school, a teacher had said that much of the ocean remains a mystery and that there could be unknown animals living in its depths. *No thanks*, Kelly had thought. She didn't want to know what other people-eating monsters lived in the sea. A swimming pool with clear water, a diving board, and lounge chairs was just fine with her. And if all that wasn't bad enough, they would be sailing through the Bermuda Triangle. She had seen at least three different television shows about how planes and ships had disappeared in the Bermuda Triangle. The trip had been a stupid idea even then and look where she was now, floating all alone in the ocean in a raging storm—and in the Bermuda Triangle, no less.

Through her tears and the blowing sea spray, Kelly saw a flash of white about twenty feet to her left. She swam toward it, thinking that it might be the boat. She kicked hard and pulled as if in a race.

Her heart sank when she realized it wasn't the boat. But it was a life buoy. She grabbed it and held on with a grip so tight her fingers hurt. At least now she had something to hang onto, something to help her float. But still she was all alone in the ocean in a storm. No boat, no land, and no one else anywhere in sight.

Tears ran down her face as Kelly strained her eyes looking for the boat.

"I'm over here! Help! Mom! Dad! I'm here!" she yelled. *"I'm over here!"*

~   ~   ~

It had taken precious minutes for Thomas to explain to his parents what had happened. In the storm, they couldn't lower the small boat that was strapped to the back of the sailboat to search for Kelly. They would have to carefully turn the large sailboat around, and that took time, valuable time. The longer it took to turn the boat, the farther away they would be from where Kelly had gone over. Her father knew that the wind and waves were dragging his daughter away and the chances of finding her in the wild sea were diminishing quickly. From a boat, even in calm weather, it was hard to spot a person floating in the water. At least Thomas had tossed the life buoy in the direction Kelly had fallen. And she was an excellent swimmer. But time was running out on the Wickmers and their daughter, who was now struggling for her life.

3

The Wickmer family searched for hours. They motored back and forth, over and over in the area where they had encountered the storm. They had been sailing for five hours since leaving Grand Bahama when the storm blew in. They were planning to pick up the strong ocean current known as the Gulf Stream to help push them further north on their way to Bermuda.

Most of the bad weather had now passed, leaving behind a dull gray sky and waves about four to five feet high. The mood aboard the sailboat had become somber. What was to be a dream vacation had turned into a horrible nightmare.

"Kelly! Kelly!" yelled Mrs. Wickmer, more quietly muttering, "Where are you?"

"We'll find her. We've got to," said Mr. Wickmer, staring through the binoculars.

"I should have grabbed her or dove in after her," sobbed Thomas.

"There was no way you could have done that, son," said Mr. Wickmer, giving his son a reassuring pat on the back. "The wave knocked us all off our feet. Thank god we were wearing harnesses."

"But…but I teased her about sharks when we went snorkeling and then I called her a baby when the storm hit."

"Thomas, throwing that life buoy was very good, quick thinking. It might just save her life. It's not your fault."

James Wickmer had already called in a mayday on the radio and gotten word to the U.S. Coast Guard. They would start a search from the air and sea as soon as they could get a plane, a helicopter, or a ship into the area, but it would take hours just to get there.

~   ~   ~

After several hours of crying, yelling for help, and hanging onto the ring buoy, Kelly was exhausted. Her voice was hoarse and she had no tears left to shed. The seas had calmed, but the adrenaline that had previously coursed through her body and given her energy was now gone. She was scared, alone, and more tired than she had ever been in her life.

Kelly's eyelids grew droopy. No, she couldn't fall asleep. How would she hang on until her parents found her? She had to stay awake. But she was just so tired. Her eyes closed and she fell asleep, drifting aimlessly in the sea. Somehow she managed to stay draped across the floating life ring.

When Kelly woke up, she was sure she had been having a terrible nightmare about falling off their rented sailboat. She would open her eyes and be in the cramped bunk on the boat, and her mom would be cooking dinner in the ship's tiny kitchen. Instead, she woke up shivering, floating on a life buoy in the open ocean, all alone. It hit her all over again—there had been a storm, and a wave had swept her off the boat. Why hadn't they found her by now? Where were the boat and her parents? She sobbed silently.

She thought back to when they had been in the Bahamas. Almost every afternoon the family would go snorkeling, all except Kelly, that is. Her brother would jump in with his mask, fins, and snorkel and put his hand up like a fin, loudly humming the ominous music from the movie *Jaws*—*dunt, dunt…dunt, dunt*—just to scare her.

Her parents kept trying to get her to go in, but she could just imagine a shark swimming up from the dark depths below. She didn't want to go in the ocean. And she definitely didn't want to go in with a mask on and actually see what was going to eat her. She tightened her grip on the life buoy, trying not to think of the sharks that were surely swimming just out of sight.

The sun was going down and soon it would be dark. Before long, the blackness in the ocean below would be all around her. Her head ached, in fact everything hurt, and she was thirsty—really thirsty. She imagined a tall glass of lemonade and thought of her friends back home. Why had they gone on this stupid trip! If she could just hang on longer, they had to find her. Her father used to be in the Navy; he'd find her. She just had to hang on and try not to be scared.

The sun went down and darkness surrounded Kelly. She thought how very black it was, no lights anywhere. Was that movement she saw to her left? Was it a fin, like in all those movies? Kelly shook with fright and closed her eyes.

At least the wind and waves had calmed. There was just a slight breeze and small rolling hills of water. She took a deep breath and slowly opened her eyes. Suddenly, a dazzling display of shimmering light exploded in a nearby wave. Kelly shook her head, thinking maybe she had fallen asleep again and was dreaming. There it was again. Only this time the sparkling looked like flashes of blue-green and dancing sparks. It was moving toward her. All at once her fear became overwhelming. Panicking, she tried to swim away from the shimmering light. She kicked and kicked, but holding onto the life buoy made swimming awkward. What was it? Would it eat her? Maybe it had something to do with being in the Bermuda Triangle.

The sparkling light was now even closer. Kelly turned away and closed her eyes again. If she didn't look, maybe it would go away. Then she heard a clicking, squeaking sound and a sort of *poof.* Her curiosity got the best of her, and she opened her eyes to a squint, slowly looking back. There on a small wave rolling toward her, surrounded by shimmering blue-green light, was a large dolphin. She had only seen dolphins on television and they never glowed. It looked like an underwater angel.

The glowing dolphin swam right past Kelly. As it went by, she briefly saw the animal's large dark eye. It looked right at her and she could swear the dolphin was smiling. The sleek beast then turned around in a flash of green and came toward her again. This time it slowed as it came closer and its halo of blue-green light dimmed. The dolphin was so near that Kelly tentatively reached out and felt its smooth, rubbery skin. Once again it passed by. In its glow, Kelly saw water spout from a hole atop the animal's head, making the *poof* sound. On its third pass, the dolphin dove down just before reaching her and disappeared. Kelly swiveled around, looking for the glowing creature.

A few moments later the dolphin rose up beneath the life buoy, and before Kelly could even wonder what was happening, the ring was hooked on the dolphin's fin. She didn't know if she should let go or hang on. She kept her grip and was soon gliding effortlessly through the sea. All around her the water was shimmering blue-green. It was like being surrounded by thousands of twinkling stars. She couldn't believe it. Maybe she was dreaming after all. Where was the dolphin going? Would it take her to her parents? The eye had looked kind.

To Kelly it seemed as if the ride lasted for hours. It was as though she had turned into the dolphin that was now spiriting her through the sea, surrounded by dancing lights. At one point she and the buoy had slipped off the animal's fin. Amazingly, the dolphin had stopped, turned around, and slid its fin into the ring again. She forgot about being scared or feeling cold, tired, or even thirsty.

A little while later the dolphin slowed and dove down, turning slightly on its side. The life buoy slid off the animal's fin. Kelly was once again afloat and alone. When she tried to get a better grip on the buoy her feet unexpectedly hit the bottom. She was in shallow water. The dolphin came back and with its beak pushed Kelly into even shallower water. She was on a beach. With the very last of her strength she crawled out of the water and lay face down in the sand. She looked back at the ocean and saw the dolphin once more. Kelly gave a brief wave and mumbled, "Thank you," before falling sound asleep.

---- **4** ----

Someone was shaking her.

"Hey, get up, get up. Are you okay?"

Kelly thought it must be Thomas or her mother waking her for school. But when she opened her eyes, she knew it wasn't so. She was lying on the sand and there was a strange boy staring down at her. He was about her height, skinny, with short red-brown hair that stuck out in all directions. He was wearing nothing but funny-looking blue shorts or maybe it was a skirt.

Kelly tried to answer, but her throat and mouth were so dry all that came out was a croaking sound.

"I'm Jack, who are you? Where'd you come from? How'd you get here? Are you hurt?" asked the boy, speaking very fast.

Kelly turned over and sat up. Just as she glanced up to get a better look at the boy named Jack, a group of people came running down the beach. She was sure they were people, but they didn't look like anyone she had ever seen. The first thing she noticed was their eyes—they were brown, but sort of cloudy. She remembered seeing pictures in a book of people with an eye disease—their eyes had looked similar. These people also had skin that looked different; it was mocha-colored, but kind of shiny in the sun.

A woman about her mother's age was one of the first to reach her.

"Jack, give the girl some room," she said. "Honey, are you okay?"

"I…I think so," answered Kelly in a raspy, hoarse voice. "Where am I?"

The woman bending over her had long wavy red-brown hair the same color as the boy's. It was tied loosely in a ponytail. She was built sturdily and her face was pleasant with high rosy cheeks and wide, full lips. She had the same cloudy brown eyes and shiny skin as the others.

"Give her some room," said the woman, shooing the others away. "You're safe now. Are you hurt?"

Kelly tried to stand up, but her legs were like rubber. A tall man standing nearby eyed her suspiciously. In fact, Kelly thought some of the other people were looking at her oddly as well.

"Take her up to my place," ordered the woman. "Jack, you come along, and the rest of you look around for any wreckage or others."

The man nearby stepped over and picked Kelly up with ease. He carried her up the beach with the woman and the boy, Jack, trailing behind. The man's hair was the same red-brown shade as the others and it was cropped short like Jack's. His face was narrow and he had thin lips set in a definite scowl, which made Kelly wonder if she had done something wrong. Maybe she was trespassing by being on the beach.

As the man carried her, Kelly took a closer look at Jack. He looked about her age, maybe a little older. He had the same shiny, light brown skin as the others and big round brown eyes that were only slightly cloudy.

As the boy followed, a running dialogue of questions spewed from his mouth. "Where'd you come from? How'd you get here—was it a big ship or an airplane? And what about…"

"Jack, give it a rest," said the woman, shaking her head. "We'll find all of that out in good time."

Kelly smiled; she sounded a lot like her mother. And then she thought about her mom. Where was she? She was probably really angry with Kelly for coming up on deck in the storm. Thoughts of her mother faded though when she entered the village.

Like the people, the village was unlike anything Kelly had ever seen, except maybe in the movies. Everything was made of a beautiful white stone that shone brilliantly in the bright morning sun. There were many small houses built of it. Shiny round balls of it lined sandy walkways and surrounded gardens of brightly colored flowers. There were bushes and vines, lush with pink and purple flowers, and trees with curved green tops that had big red blooms hanging down. There were also many large sculptures made from the same lustrous white rock. Sparkling stone dolphins, sharks, sea turtles, and large rays adorned the walkways and gardens. Kelly realized there were no paved roads and she saw no cars. Where was she? It was the most beautiful place she had ever seen.

By now, many of the villagers had gathered around and were watching and whispering as Kelly was carried up to one of the small white stone homes. The doorway was an arch of white rock covered by a twisting vine with long, yellow bell-shaped flowers. A wooden door with a carving of a dolphin on it stood open, letting the air and light flow freely inside.

With a few strides of his long legs, the man carried Kelly through the house into a small bedroom. From what she saw, it was obvious that this home was very different than her own back in Massachusetts.

A high thatched roof sat atop the home's white stone walls. The furniture was all made from wood or vines, and an abundance of tropical plants decorated the rooms. There were green ferns and pink flowers growing in the walls, and she could have sworn she saw a tree in the living room. It looked as if nature itself had created the house. In the bedroom she saw beautiful seashells of all shapes and sizes. A woven mat lined the floor, and baskets lay scattered about the room. Over the bed hung a painting of a dolphin leaping out of the water.

Without saying a word, the tall man set her down on the bed and headed for the door.

"Surge, go get Pearl," said the woman from the beach, coming in behind them. "She'll need to take a look at her."

The man scowled more intensely, sighed loudly, and then nodded ever so slightly and left.

"What's your name, honey? We've got a doctor coming. Would you like some water?"

"My name's Kelly…Kelly Wickmer. Yes, water please," she croaked. Her throat was very dry.

"Jack, go get her some water," said the woman to the boy, who stood in the doorway watching.

"I'm Sharly Pesca and you've already met my son, Jack. Does anything hurt? Are you injured?"

Jack came in holding a cup made from the hard, dark-brown inside shell of a coconut and handed it to Kelly. The water inside tasted incredibly cool and sweet.

"More, please," she said.

As Jack left to get more, Kelly looked up at Mrs. Pesca with tears in her eyes.

"I fell off the boat. There was a big storm. My parents must be really mad and looking for me."

"Kelly, it's okay, you're safe now. Can you move your arms and legs? Looks like you may have hit your head. There's a large bump just above your eyebrow."

Kelly reached up to feel the bump.

"*Ouch. M*ust've hit it when I fell off the boat."

Just then a slender woman, hardly taller than Kelly, came through the door. She had wavy red-brown hair that fell just below her shoulders. She was wearing a green cloth draped around her body. As she got closer, Kelly noticed that her cloudy brown eyes were slanted at their outer edges and rimmed with long, dark eyelashes. She thought the woman was pretty, though her pursed mouth currently lent her a somewhat dour expression.

"Is this our latest arrival?" asked the woman briskly. "Okay, stand back and let me have a look at her."

"Don't go dramatic on me, Pearl," responded Mrs. Pesca with a bit of disdain. "She looks pretty good—just some bumps and bruises."

"I'll be the judge of that."

She had Kelly move her arms and legs. Then she poked and prodded her, including the bump on her head, which made Kelly flinch.

"She'll be fine with some rest and water. If you need me, you know where to find me."

And before Kelly could even say thank you, the woman strode out the door and was gone. Mrs. Pesca looked down at Kelly with her large, cloudy brown eyes and a kindness the woman doctor had not shown.

"You've been through quite an ordeal. It's amazing, really. Looks like you have only some bumps and bruises to show for it. Let's get you some more water, a little rest, and some dry clothes."

Kelly remembered falling off the boat and the storm, but how she had gotten to the beach was a bit foggy. She wasn't sure what had really happened. Maybe she had just floated there and dreamed of the angel dolphin. But where was *there*? Where was she?

5

After getting Kelly more water, Mrs. Pesca helped her to take a shower and put on a beautiful blue-and-white wrap of cloth decorated with the outlines of dolphins. She showed her how to put it on. The material was unfamiliar to Kelly; it was almost like cotton but kind of stretchy, like a bathing suit.

"That's just one way to wear it," said Mrs. Pesca. "I'll show you some other ways later. We also have two-piece outfits that will look just lovely on you."

"Where am I? Can I call my parents to let them know I'm okay?" asked Kelly.

"Have a little rest and then if you're feeling well enough, Jack can show you around."

Though Kelly was only twelve years old, she wondered why the woman hadn't answered her question.

"What about calling my parents?"

"We can talk about that later…rest for now."

The older woman got up and walked out of the room. Kelly was very tired, and as soon as she lay down, she fell asleep.

Kelly slept for a few hours, but it was a restless sleep. She dreamed of being back in the stormy ocean at night, surrounded by blackness. A fin approached and she screamed, trying to swim away. She imagined the jagged teeth of a shark about to gobble her up. Then she heard someone calling her name and felt a hand on her shoulder. She opened her eyes to find the boy, Jack, standing over her.

"Kelly, Kelly, wake up, you're having a nightmare."

She closed her eyes and opened them again, remembering where she was. A tear trickled down her cheek.

"Ahh, I think you were dreaming," said Jack, shuffling his feet awkwardly. "Don't worry. My mom says you're going to be okay."

Kelly shook her head, rubbing the sleep and tears from her eyes.

"I was back in the ocean and I think there was a shark. I really need to call my parents to let them know I'm okay, and so they can come get me."

The boy looked away, avoiding her eyes.

"I can show you around if you want," he said.

"Where am I anyway?"

Jack smiled and this time, looked directly at her.

"You're on Dolphin Island," he answered proudly.

Kelly looked doubtingly at him.

"Dolphin Island? I don't remember seeing that on the chart. My dad showed me all the islands around here."

"Well, it's not really on charts or maps," said Jack a little awkwardly.

"What do you mean not on maps? All islands are on maps. There are people who do that for a living. You know, draw maps and things. Now, they even use satellites and computers to make it right. I've read about it in books and my dad told me."

"Hey, I'm just telling you like it is," responded Jack, throwing his hands up in the air. "You asked, I answered. You're on Dolphin Island, the best place around."

Kelly was going to respond, but just then she noticed something really weird about Jack's hands. There was skin between his fingers, sort of like a duck's feet—they were webbed. Jack saw Kelly staring at his hands.

"Come on," he said, turning toward the door. "Let's go."

Kelly was so surprised at his hands that she forgot what she was going to say and wasn't sure what to say next. She was also a bit confused from all that had happened, so she just followed the boy out the door. She noticed that the wrap around his waist was similar to the one she had on, only it was decorated with sharks, not dolphins.

Outside it was warm and sunny—nothing like the day before. Kelly didn't want to think about the storm, drifting in the ocean, or her parents. So she just followed Jack, listening as he played tour guide. He was talking very fast.

"Over here, that's our garden and look up at the roof—see how it's made so that rain runs off and goes into that container? That's so we can collect it. See the stand of coconut trees over there and the banana trees over there. And look at the top of our tree sticking out of the house."

Kelly saw something large scurry across the sand.

"*AARGH!* I'll get you this time!" yelled Jack, sprinting after it.

She followed hesitantly and found Jack standing over a large hole by the side of his house, cursing under his breath.

"What's down there?" she asked curiously.

"It's one of those darn land crabs. Big one, too. They come out at night mostly, but this one likes to torment me during the day. I swear I'm going to catch it and then…it'll be soup!"

"Land crabs? I thought crabs lived in the ocean," said Kelly looking into the hole, but not seeing a crab or anything else.

"Some do, but these live on land…you'll see 'em. Pretty harmless, except when you try to catch 'em—big claws, you know," boasted Jack with a tone that implied he'd caught a lot of the large crabs before.

Kelly looked at the skinny boy in front of her with his wild hair sticking out in all directions and somehow couldn't imagine him wrestling large-clawed crabs or anything else for that matter. In fact, the idea was rather funny, and she had to stop herself from snickering.

Near the crab's hole, surrounding a small flowerbed beside Jack's house, were some of the round white rocks that lined the village's walkways. Kelly looked at one of them more closely and noticed a strange pattern in the rock; there were little cup-like depressions all over it, each with a small star of ridges at the center.

"What kind of rock is that?" she asked, pointing to the odd round stone.

"Why that, it's a coral, of course," answered Jack, looking at Kelly as if she knew nothing.

"You may have land crabs, but even I know that corals live underwater."

"It's not a live coral," said Jack smugly. "That's the skeleton of a really, really old, dead one."

Kelly was beginning to dislike Jack's know-it-all tone.

"You see all this white rock around here?" said Jack. "It comes from a cliff that used to be a coral reef living underwater. Now it's rock, but you can still see the shapes of corals that used to live there."

"See this?" said Jack, pointing to a rock that was part of the outside wall of his home. "It's, well, it used to be, a branching coral."

It looked as if someone had made a large impression of a fan in the stone.

"Kind of like a fossil, I guess," said Kelly, "but how did the coral reef get in the cliff?"

"It's got something to do with either the ocean getting lower or the land getting higher," replied Jack, scratching his head. He didn't sound quite as smug as before. "We learned about it in school, but I can never remember which it is. It's either that the ocean was higher a long time ago and then got lower or an earthquake lifted the land up. Either way, the reef died and now it's part of the cliff. But if you think that's cool, wait till I show you some of the other stuff around here."

And with that, Jack ran ahead toward the beach.

Kelly didn't quite know what to make of Jack or her surroundings, but she did know that she was tired and sore. She let Jack go ahead, following at a slower pace. She was walking down a wide sandy path lined by the round white rocks. Looking closer, she saw that each stone had tiny cup-like depressions and star-shaped ridges—they were all old, dead corals. She never knew that corals looked like rocks when they were dead, but then again, she wasn't really sure what they looked like when they were alive either.

Looking around, Kelly saw people of all ages busily tending their gardens and the trees that seemed to grow out of each house. Some of the bigger homes had two trees sprouting from the roof. Then she heard a gurgling sound. Glancing down to her feet, she saw that the sandy path had become a little wooden bridge crossing over a small stream that flowed through the village. Now that she looked closer, a few of the houses had streams running through or under them. Some even had small waterfalls coming out of the sides of the house.

As Kelly walked, she also noticed tall trees laden with fruit. She recognized avocados on a tree in one yard and mangoes on another. There was also an odd-looking tree with fruit she didn't recognize. The tree was tall with a very skinny grayish trunk and almost no branches. At the top, there were a few large droopy leaves with fat green fruits hanging below. Those weren't the only fruits she didn't know—on another tree she saw weird dark-green, football-shaped fruits with spiky skin. On one plant, she recognized small red peppers, but they were growing upside down, their skinny ends pointing skyward.

As Kelly passed, people turned her way, staring and nodding; others eyed her suspiciously. They all wore wraps much like hers but in lots of different colors and patterns. Some were one-piece and fit loosely, while others were two-piece and fit tighter. She tried not to stare back, but just couldn't help herself. They all had webbed hands like Jack. Their eyes were cloudy, particularly the older people, and when they turned just right in the sun their skin seemed to shimmer. Kelly didn't want to be rude by gawking at them, and their stares made her feel uncomfortable, so she headed more quickly in the direction Jack had gone.

She caught up with him at the beach. Jack was talking to a girl who was shorter than Kelly with long, red-brown hair that was tied in a ponytail high atop her head. She had a small nose, a cute round face, and brown eyes that were only slightly cloudy.

"Kelly, this is Paroe Aguan. Paroe, this is Kelly Wickmer," said Jack very formally.

"Hi," said Kelly.

She wanted to ask them about their hands and eyes, but decided it might be rude.

"I'm twelve, how old are you?" she asked instead.

"I'm thirteen," answered Jack quickly. "Paroe's eleven."

Kelly figured Paroe would never get a word in with fast-talking Jack around.

"Have you lived here long, Paroe?"

"I've always lived here," she replied in a quiet, calm voice.

"We've all always lived here," said Jack, shaking his head, looking as if it had been the dumbest question he'd ever heard.

Kelly didn't think it was a stupid question.

"Haven't you ever visited other places?"

"Nope, no reason to," replied Jack.

"You've never gone away on vacation, seen other places, new things?"

"Nope," said Jack simply, shaking his head again and heading down the beach. "You'll see. C'mon, let's go to the sea pools."

Paroe stayed behind.

"Don't take Jack too seriously," she whispered.

Kelly smiled, feeling a little less put off.

"I've just never seen a place like this before. It's very different than where I come from."

Paroe seemed about to say something else, when Jack hollered back for them to catch up.

Paroe smiled and ran ahead. Kelly followed. It was the first time she had seen the ocean since the dolphin brought her to the beach—or had it? She was still unsure about what had really happened the previous night.

As she walked, Kelly gazed out over the water; it was a spectacular view. They were on a white sandy beach that sloped gradually down to calm, crystal-clear water. As she looked seaward, Kelly thought the water was an unusual shade of blue. It wasn't the navy blue or green color she was used to at home in Massachusetts or even what she had seen while sailing. Here the water was a color she never imagined the ocean could be. With the sun above and just a few clouds in the sky, the ocean appeared a brilliant shade of aqua blue. Some might even call it turquoise. Kelly thought it was prettier than any paint or crayon color she had ever seen.

Three brown pelicans then soared by one after another in a high-flying game of follow-the-leader. Their long bills were stretched forward and their large wings spread wide as they glided by, riding on invisible currents in the air.

In the distance, Kelly could see a few boats; they looked like wide canoes. One of the boats had a small, white triangular sail up and was skimming along the ocean's surface. There were two or three people with each boat; some were swimming, others were standing or sitting. Behind the canoes, farther in the distance, a line of white seemed to encircle the island for as far as she could see. Then she heard Jack calling her name.

"See the pools?" said Jack, when Kelly reached him. He was pointing just ahead where the island curved around and disappeared behind a dark rocky cliff.

Kelly was mesmerized by what lay ahead. At the base of a small cliff, there were three round pools of water, each about fifteen feet across. Walls of black rock created a barrier between each pool as well as the ocean. A man stood next to the pools with a long wooden pole. But what really grabbed Kelly's attention were the three large dolphins swimming side by side toward the pools.

Kelly could see their light gray, smooth skin. They were swimming fast with each of the dolphin's fins just above the water and their beaks surging forward.

"What are those dolphins doing? Are they going to hit the rocks?" asked Kelly.

"Oh, just wait, you'll see," said Jack, and Paroe nodded knowingly.

As they got closer the dolphins spread out slightly. When they were only about two feet from the rocks, a school of short, silvery fish jumped up in front of the dolphins. The fish landed right in the pools and the dolphins instantly swerved away. All three in unison then leapt high into the air, twirled, and landed with a tremendous splash. The man standing by the pools got drenched. Then he gave a dramatic, though soggy, bow.

"*Wow!*" exclaimed Kelly.

Jack laughed and Paroe clapped her hands in appreciation for the dolphins.

"The dolphins help us fish," said Jack. "See, watch the man over there. That's Sundy. He's the fishkeeper."

As Kelly watched, the man named Sundy took the long pole he was holding and dipped it into one of the pools. A net on the end came up holding several fish.

He then bowed to the dolphins once more and said, "Thank you, my friends."

Sundy tossed a fish into the air. In an instant, one of the dolphins jumped up and snatched the fish in midair. Two more fish were thrown and the other two dolphins did the very same thing. Then with a flick of their tails, all three dolphins turned and disappeared beneath the water's surface. Kelly thought she heard a sound that seemed familiar, a sort of clicking, squeaking noise.

Jack and Paroe turned toward Kelly with broad smiles, seeing the amazement in her eyes.

"Other people here fish with spears or nets, but the dolphins help us too," explained Jack. "The creatures of the sea help us and we help them. Last year, two dolphins were stranded on the beach and we helped them get back into the water. And just the other day, one of the spearfishers untangled a big barracuda from an old fishing net."

Kelly couldn't really believe it.

"*A barracuda?* Didn't it bite him? Like…like a shark would?" she asked.

"Barracudas are fine," answered Jack, shrugging nonchalantly. "They have territories—so if you're in their territory, they follow you around. Look kinda scary, but they don't usually bite. And sharks are cool, as long as you don't mess with them. I've swum with a ton of them, and once, I had to wrestle a big shark for a fish I had speared."

Paroe rolled her eyes and snickered.

"What? What?" questioned Jack with a smirk.

"People aren't really good shark food," said Paroe, ignoring Jack. "They like to eat fish. When people get bitten, it's usually just a mistake. Like the time a shark tried to eat a fish a guy had speared and got his foot instead. But as soon as it bit the guy, the shark spit him out. I don't think he tasted very good."

"Well, I sure hope I don't taste very good," said Kelly. "What about the other things in the ocean, like jellyfish? Don't they sting you?"

"They'll only sting if you run into them," replied Paroe. "Jellyfish can't really swim very well. So it's just bad luck if you bump into one without seeing it."

"But they must be hard to see, especially if you don't have on swim goggles or a mask."

"We don't need those," declared Jack.

"Really? In the pool when I open my eyes underwater everything looks all blurry," said Kelly.

"Our eyes let us see better underwater," explained Paroe.

Kelly didn't want to be rude, but she was just so curious.

"Is that why your eyes are sort of cloudy?" she asked a bit hesitantly.

Jack pointed to Paroe's eyes.

"Yeah, our eyes look more like yours now, but as we get older and spend more time in the water, they'll get cloudier."

Kelly figured she might as well ask the other burning question.

"What about your hands?"

"Figured you had noticed," answered Jack, spreading his fingers apart. "We've got webbed hands and feet for better swimming. It's no big deal really. Let's go look in the pools."

To them it may have been no big deal, but for Kelly, having webbed hands and feet, as well as cloudy eyes that can see underwater, was extremely strange. Again she wondered just where she was.

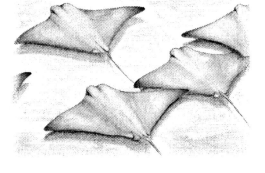

6

They walked closer to the pools for a better view. The fishkeeper, Sundy, was netting the fish that had landed in the outer pools and putting them all into the middle one. The fish were short and silvery. They reminded Kelly of the sardines her dad liked to eat on toast for breakfast. She thought it was really gross. He ate nearly the whole thing—the guts, tail, and even the skin.

Kelly looked into the outer pool to the right. There were at least a hundred large shellfish scattered over the bottom. She had no idea what they were, but every once in a while one would jump up, madly flap its shell, and shoot forward. Or maybe it was going backward?

"What are those?" she asked.

"Well, little lady, those are scallops," answered Sundy, the fishkeeper. "Haven't you ever seen a scallop before?"

Kelly looked up. Sundy was an odd-looking man. He was quite fat around the middle, had a large nose, and was completely bald. There wasn't a stitch of hair on his head; it all seemed to have migrated to his eyebrows, as they were unbelievably thick and bushy. Kelly thought they looked a lot like huge brown caterpillars. She might have been scared of Sundy, but his voice was very kind.

"I've seen scallops on my plate, but never in the shell or the water. I didn't know they could swim like that."

"Yup, quick little suckers once they get going," said the fishkeeper, nodding hello to Jack and Paroe. "And you must be Kelly, our new arrival. Pleased to meet you. I'm Sundy."

"Hi," replied Kelly a bit shyly.

"Want to see what's in the other pool?"

Kelly nodded.

Sundy stepped over to the pool on the opposite side of the one holding the small silvery fish. Even with his rather wide girth, he moved with surprising ease over the rocks.

"Right now this one has lobster and conch in it," he told them. "The conch are the ones sitting still with the big thick shells. If you look closely, you can see their stalked eyes poking out from under the shell. The other creatures, the ones with lots of legs and the long spines waving in front, those are the lobsters. Maybe you've seen them before? I feel bad keeping them cooped up like this, but at least for now they're well fed and happy."

"How do you know they're happy?" asked Kelly.

Sundy contemplated for a minute before answering.

"Well, it seems to me that in the ocean, animals spend their time finding food, trying not to be eaten by bigger animals, and searching for a mate. So I figure two out of three isn't bad—I feed them, so they've got food, and at the moment no one is trying to eat them." He winked and added, "And who knows, maybe they fool around a little when I'm not looking."

Sundy let out a booming laugh and his caterpillar eyebrows danced up and down. Kelly, Jack, and Paroe couldn't help but laugh as well.

"Hey there, Miss Paroe, how's my fellow animal-lover doing these days?" asked Sundy, looking fondly at the other girl.

"Fine, thanks," answered Paroe, blushing slightly.

"I'm not supposed to keep Kelly away too long," announced Jack. "We'd better head back."

The three of them said good-bye to the fishkeeper and walked back along the beach the way they had come.

Jack walked in front of the other two. He rambled on about things on the island, including the ponds where they grew algae for food. Picturing the green slime that she'd seen growing on the walls of a friend's glass aquarium, Kelly hoped they didn't have algae for dinner.

They were nearly back in front of the village when Paroe pointed into the water.

"Look, the rays are here," she shouted excitedly, running down to the water's edge.

Kelly stared into the shallow water where Paroe was pointing. There must have been over thirty small rays swimming about. Each was light brown in color, about a foot across, and diamond shaped, with a short, blunt snout and a long whip-like tail.

Before she could say anything, Jack and Paroe were standing in the water among the swimming sea creatures.

"C'mon Kelly, it's great—they're really friendly," said Paroe as she put her hand down and stroked the top of one of the rays. Another came over and nuzzled her leg affectionately.

Kelly stood frozen in place.

"I...I think I'll just watch from here. They're stingrays, aren't they?"

"Very dangerous," pronounced Jack in a particularly serious tone. Then he jumped in and swam with the creatures.

"Don't listen to him," said Paroe. "He's just kidding. They're perfectly safe. These are cownose stingrays. They only have a little needle on their tails. Just don't step on it. They won't bite. I don't think they even *have* teeth. Really, they're very friendly and they feel really soft. C'mon, try it."

Like a flock of curious underwater birds, the small rays were circling around Paroe's legs. Kelly stepped closer to the sea's edge, but she was still unsure about getting in the ocean with the creatures. It took about ten more minutes of coaxing by Paroe before Kelly got in. She stood nervously in the knee-deep water beside the other girl. The water felt cool in the day's heat, but Kelly began to lose her nerve as soon as a ray started swimming toward her. She stood as still as one could possibly stand, thinking maybe she had made a mistake. Just before she gave up and jumped out, a ray brushed her leg. Then the creature came back and nuzzled her shin. She couldn't believe it. Soon a few more rays came over and did the same thing. Kelly hesitantly reached down to touch one. To her surprise, the ray seemed to stop for her to stroke its skin. It felt like soft velvet.

Kelly giggled and looked up at Paroe.

"They're so soft," she said in amazement.

"See, we told you so," shouted Jack, swimming nearby among the rays.

The three of them spent another half hour playing with the school of cownose rays. Jack and Paroe swam with the creatures, while Kelly stayed in the shallower water and let the rays swirl around her legs. They were incredibly graceful, gliding through the water with the slow up-and-down beating of their wing-like bodies.

Afterward, as Jack walked up the beach, he turned to Kelly and said, "Pretty cool, huh?"

Kelly nodded enthusiastically. She stood looking at the rays as they swam away, a huge grin spread across her face.

They then said goodbye to Paroe and headed back into the village.

As they were approaching his house, Jack stopped abruptly and put his arm up in front of Kelly.

"Stop. See it? See the crab by the side of the house?" he whispered.

Jack was pointing to the largest crab Kelly had ever seen. It was bluish orange in color and must have been nearly a foot across. And it had two very large claws raised up on either side of its rectangular-shaped body.

Jack crouched down and tiptoed toward it. The crab shuffled a little to the side. Jack stopped for a moment, and it turned toward him as if sensing his presence.

"I've got you now!" he exclaimed, diving for the crab. But the creature darted away just in time, scurrying inside its hole. And Jack was left with nothing but a face full of sand.

Kelly tried not to laugh, but she just couldn't prevent a chuckle from escaping.

"Hey, I've caught them before," assured Jack, getting up and spitting some sand out of his mouth.

"I'm sure you have," replied Kelly, smiling.

~   ~   ~

By the time they arrived at the Pesca's house, it was late afternoon.

"Kelly, you must be exhausted," greeted Mrs. Pesca. "Why don't you lie down for a bit and then you can join us for dinner. Jack, wipe that sand off outside. Your father should be home soon."

Kelly was tired. The afternoon had worn her out.

"Okay, can I call my parents first to tell them I'm all right?"

Sharly Pesca quickly ushered her into the same small bedroom as before.

"Here you go; this can be your room. We'll talk about your parents after you've rested," she said.

As Kelly closed her eyes and drifted off to sleep, she heard Jack and his mother whispering. She thought she heard her name in the conversation.

7

Kelly wasn't sure how long she'd been asleep, but when she opened her eyes it was dark outside and a cool breeze was blowing through the house. The wind was whistling through a fine mesh that covered the windows and outside, the palm trees were rustling in the breeze. At first, the sounds brought back memories of the howling wind at sea during the storm. Kelly tensed. But it wasn't the same; the breeze was light and refreshing and she lay snuggled in a warm, soft bed. She relaxed. Then she heard voices outside the door. One was deeper than the others.

Kelly got up, straightened her hair and clothes, and went into the living room. Jack, his mother, and an older man sat talking quietly. They looked very serious. The man had the same short, messy red-brown hair and big brown eyes as Jack. His hair was going gray just behind his temples and his eyes were very cloudy. He had a square jaw, and she could see the muscles in his arms and chest. She thought he was quite handsome.

They hadn't heard her come in, so Kelly decided to take a look around. Jack and his father sat on a couch that had been carved into one of the home's stone walls. It had a thick cushion covered in light-blue cloth. Mrs. Pesca sat on a chair made from dark wood and lighter-colored vines with a similar blue cushion. There was also a dark wood coffee table decorated with carvings of sea turtles and dolphins. Beside the sitting area was the trunk of a huge tree that spread across nearly one whole side of the house. Its wide, smooth brown base and roots had to be at least six feet across. Some of the branches were inside the house and helped create the beams of the thatched roof. The rest of the tree stuck out through the roof.

Kelly heard the trickle of flowing water. Looking across the room, she saw water coming out of a hole in the wall flowing down into a rectangular basin at the floor. It was a small indoor waterfall. Kelly also noticed that the light inside was coming from candles made out of seashells and several strange-looking globes. Each odd globe gave off a soft bluish light, and every once in a while the inside sparkled.

"Oh, you're up, just in time for dinner," said Mrs. Pesca. "Kelly, this is Jack's father."

"Hello Kelly," greeted Mr. Pesca. His voice was very deep, and when he smiled, the lines around his eyes crinkled.

"Hi," said Kelly shyly.

"Hey Kelly, Dad's been out spearing," said Jack, talking as fast as ever. "Wait till you see dinner, it'll be great. Weren't those rays awesome? I knew you'd like them. Wait till tomorrow and—"

"Speaking of dinner," interrupted Mrs. Pesca. "C'mon everyone, let's sit down." She ushered them around a corner into another section of the room.

They sat down at a large round table. It was made of dark brown wood with shiny pink dolphins rimming the edges.

Mr. Pesca saw Kelly looking at the table.

"The pink dolphins are made from a conch shell," he explained, "like the one on the shelf over there."

He pointed to a set of shelves lined with seashells, including the largest one she had ever seen. It was a huge conch shell with a bumpy spiraled top and a thick, wide lip. The inside of the shell was smooth, shiny, and very pink.

Kelly looked down at her plate and silverware. The plate was a large scallop shell. It was round except on one side. The underside of the shell was grayish with narrow ridges, while the top was smooth and pearly. A shiny pink fork and spoon sat next to her plate. Their cups were also made from shells; they were golden tan in color and shaped like fat spiraling tubes. Each sat in a small wooden holder so that it would stand upright.

One of the odd light globes had been placed on the table at the middle. Mr. Pesca saw Kelly gazing quizzically at it.

"I bet you're wondering what creates the light inside the orb," he said. "The outside is made from the egg sack of a fish. After the babies are born, we collect the sacks and then clean and stretch them. We then fill each with water from a special cave. The water contains algae that produce light in the dark. Sometimes if you go down to the ocean at night and pass your hand through the water, it will glow blue-green. In our cave pool, we grow concentrated versions of the algae that cause that. Every few weeks or so, we have to replace the glowing algae water in each orb."

He reached across the table, picked up the orb, and shook it.

"See how it shimmers? The algae inside react to the water motion and sparkle."

He handed the glowing orb to Kelly and she gave it a shake. It kind of reminded her of the glass snow globe she had gotten one Christmas.

Mrs. Pesca collected their plates and went into a small kitchen.

"Hope you like seafood," she said.

The kitchen was separated from the main living room by a short, narrow stone wall about waist high. Kelly could see a pot hanging over a fire sitting in a rectangular stone basin. Mrs. Pesca stirred the pot's contents and ladled out a large portion on each plate. From the counter next to where the pot hung, she then spooned something from a large wooden bowl onto the plates. Mr. Pesca got up to help bring in the plates, which were now mounded high with food.

"Stew and seaweed salad," announced Jack. "One of my favorites. It's much better than giant clam. We had that last night." He bent over toward Kelly and whispered, "It wasn't really very good...too chewy."

"Before we begin eating, we have a tradition here to give thanks to Mother Nature," said Mr. Pesca to Kelly.

Kelly wasn't so sure she wanted to eat what was in front of her, let alone give thanks for it, but not wanting to be rude, she followed along.

Mr. Pesca bowed his head and said, "Thank you to the sea and to the Earth for providing us with this food, keeping us safe and healthy, and bringing our new friend, Kelly, to Dolphin Island."

The other three began eating and chatting about the day. Jack told them about their visit to the sea pools and the rays. Kelly looked warily at her plate. The stew looked pretty normal; she recognized chunks of fish, lobster, and even a few scallops. It was the other stuff that was questionable. Sitting next to the seafood was a mound of something that looked like slimy green strips of rubber. She tried the stew. The fish was sweet and the scallops melted in her mouth.

"So, Kelly, what do you think?" asked Jack with a very large mouthful of food. "Did you try the seaweed? It's good, isn't it? Bet the food where you come from isn't this good."

"Jack, be nice and don't talk with your mouth full," reprimanded his mother. "Where are your manners?"

"He's not using his fingers tonight," said Jack's father, winking at his son. "I'd say that's an improvement in his manners."

"Ha-ha, that's just *soooo* funny, Dad," responded Jack, rolling his eyes.

Kelly found herself enjoying the light banter among the family as they ate. She decided to try the seaweed. She tentatively put a few of the green strips into her mouth. It tasted like a cross between lettuce and green pepper, but she didn't care for the texture; it was just as rubbery as it looked.

Mrs. Pesca saw Kelly grimace as she chewed the seaweed. She picked up a small seashell from the table and passed it to her.

"Here, try a little salt—makes it a little less chewy."

"Ahh, that's okay, I think I'll stick with the stew," said Kelly.

Kelly thought it would be a good time to ask about calling her mom and dad.

"Mrs. Pesca, do you have a phone? Can I call my parents after dinner? They must be really worried."

It immediately became very quiet around the table.

"Kelly, the problem is, we have no way of contacting your parents," said Mr. Pesca. "We don't have phones, like where you live. We know you miss your mom and dad and I'm sure they are very worried about you, but unfortunately there is nothing we can do."

Kelly didn't want to cry, but her eyes began to well up with tears.

"But…but how can you not have phones?" she stuttered. "How do you contact other islands? What happens if you need something?"

Jack's mother got up and went around the table to where Kelly sat and put her arm around her.

"Kelly, I know this is hard for you," she said kindly. "But we have everything we need right here. Every once in a while someone like you lands on our island and they come to live with us. It's very nice here and people will love you."

Kelly didn't understand. The island was beautiful, but she wanted to go home. She wanted to see her mother, her father, and even her brother, Thomas. How could they not let her go home? Was she being kidnapped?

"I don't understand. I want to go home. I have to go home," cried Kelly, and she got up and ran from the table into the small bedroom where she had slept.

Jack got up to follow her, but his father stopped him.

"Jack, you stay here. Your mother will talk to her."

~   ~   ~

Mrs. Pesca found Kelly curled up on the bed. She was crying quietly.

"Kelly, I know this is very hard for you. But you have been so brave already. You made it through the storm and a night all alone out in the ocean."

"I wasn't all alone. The dolphin was there," replied Kelly angrily.

"What dolphin?" asked the older woman, sitting next to her on the bed.

"When it got dark, a dolphin came. It looked like an angel, with light all around it. It brought me here."

In her anger, Kelly had remembered everything, in vivid detail.

"We are friends with the dolphins here," said Mrs. Pesca. "I bet the one that helped you thought you should come to our island. It knew you would like living with us."

Kelly didn't understand why she couldn't go home.

"Mrs. Pesca, can I take an airplane or a boat to another island where they have phones?"

"No, Kelly, I'm sorry but we don't have any airplanes, and by boat we cannot get through the coral reef that encircles the island. It is very dangerous. Everyone who has tried to go across the reef has either disappeared or has been very badly hurt. A few people have even died."

"Don't you want to visit other places?"

Mrs. Pesca shook her head.

"We've heard from people like you that have landed here by accident about what other places are like. Sure, we are curious, but the thought of leaving and never coming back is just too awful. And it is very dangerous. Besides, this is a wonderful place. Here we live with the sea and the Earth, as part of them really, and want for nothing. We have all the food and shelter we need, and people look out for one another."

"But there are good things in other places too. Like computers or television or cars. Don't you want any of those things?"

"There are some people who would like to see them. But if one tried to leave, it would mean getting seriously hurt or never coming back. And most of us just could not bear the thought of never seeing Dolphin

Island again. We are happy without those other things and love living here with our family, our friends, and the sea."

"But I'm not from here. I live in Massachusetts with my family. Isn't there anyone who will take me in a boat to another island?" pleaded Kelly.

"I'm so sorry, Kelly, but trying to cross the reef is just too dangerous. There isn't anyone here who will risk getting hurt or leaving forever."

Kelly still didn't completely understand.

"How come this island isn't on any maps? Why can't you see it from a boat or a plane?"

"You know, there are some things that even us grown-ups don't quite understand," said Mrs. Pesca. "We don't know why the island seems to be hidden from the rest of the world and why at times people who are lost or shipwrecked find their way here. Some people think the dolphins protect the island and only bring very special people, like you, here to live. Others say it is God's way of preserving a place that is in harmony with the Earth."

She covered Kelly with a blanket.

"That's enough for now. Get a good night's sleep, and if you want, we can talk about it some more in the morning. You will grow to like it here, I promise," she said, kissing Kelly on the forehead.

Once Mrs. Pesca had gone, Kelly lay in bed thinking about what she had said. She did think the island was beautiful, and the people seemed friendly enough. But she didn't understand how no one could know about Dolphin Island. If she had to stay, she would never see her parents, her brother, or her friends ever again. She lay softly crying and thinking about home and the strange island that she was now stuck on.

After about an hour or so, Kelly decided she was sick of crying, sick of being afraid. She was tired of feeling helpless and inept, and relying on others to help her. Jack's mother had been right. She had survived the storm, had drifted all alone in the ocean, and had swum with a dolphin. She had even stood in the water with a school of stingrays. She decided that from then on, she'd be brave. And she'd try to find a way to go home.

8

The next morning, Kelly woke up to the birds singing and sunlight streaming in through the window. It was early and the air was cool. Instead of lying in bed thinking about home and her parents, Kelly stood up, her fists clenched in determination. There just had to be a way off the island and she had to find it.

Mrs. Pesca had left a pile of clothes for her in a basket near the foot of the bed. She chose a two-piece red-and-white wrap decorated with fish. It fit tighter than the one-piece wrap, almost like one of her swimsuits, but it was more comfortable. Kelly quietly left the room and went down a short hallway to the bathroom. There were two other rooms along the hall. One door was open and she peeked in. It was the master bedroom where Jack's parents slept. The door to the other room was closed. She figured it was Jack's room. Kelly went into the small bathroom, where she washed her face and brushed her teeth. Mrs. Pesca had given her an odd-looking toothbrush—a stick with a dark yellow sponge on the end.

The toothpaste tasted a little salty, and the soap, which sat in a white clamshell with wide ridges, smelled like flowers.

When Mrs. Pesca saw that Kelly was up and dressed, she came over and gave her a big hug.

"Good morning, dear," she said cheerily. "I thought you might want to sleep in. As usual, Jack's still in bed. He'd sleep right till noon if I let him. How are you doing this morning?"

"Okay, I guess. Kind of hungry," replied Kelly.

"Now that's something I can fix. C'mon over here and have a seat. I'll get you some breakfast."

Kelly didn't want to talk about her parents or about looking for a way off of the island.

"It's not seaweed again, is it?" she asked.

"Oh, we never have seaweed at breakfast," laughed Mrs. Pesca. "How about some eggs, fruit, and a tall glass of milk?"

"Okay. Do you have a grocery store here? Where you buy your food?"

"No, but we have tortoises and goats. We raise them on the island. The tortoises provide the eggs and the goats supply the milk. We have to watch those goats though; when they escape the pens, they trample all over everything. They'll eat just about anything and simply ruin the gardens."

In Kelly's resolve to be braver, she decided that no matter how bad the tortoise eggs and goat's milk tasted she would eat them. But it wasn't the eggs or even the milk that tasted bad. Along with some scrambled eggs, Mrs. Pesca put several slices of fruit on her scallop shell plate. There were two orangey yellow slices and several chunks more reddish in color. Kelly ate the orangey fruit, recognizing the pleasant taste of mango. However, before she even bit into the reddish fruit she knew it was going to be bad. It smelled terrible, kind of like vomit. One bite and she couldn't help but make a face—it tasted like vomit too. She looked around for somewhere to spit it out, but Mrs. Pesca was looking right at her, so she closed her eyes and swallowed.

"I guess you didn't care for the papaya," chuckled Mrs. Pesca. "You don't have to eat it."

"*Phew.* It tastes really, really bad," said Kelly, relieved.

Just then, Jack showed up wearing the same wrap he had on the previous day. His hair was even messier than before, if that was possible.

"Hey, what's all the noise out here? I'm trying to sleep. It's early, for god's sake. What are you guys laughing about? Did I miss something?"

"Good morning, Jack. Sit down and give that mouth of yours a rest," said Mrs. Pesca. "Kelly here was just trying some of the papaya from our garden."

"*Ugh,* you gave her papaya. That stuff is *nasty.* Mom's always trying to get me to eat it. Even cooks it in other things thinking I won't notice. *Yuck!*"

"Oh, come on now. It's not all that bad. Your father and I like it. And the tree is simply bursting with fruit."

"Give it away, *pul...ease,*" pleaded Jack.

Despite everything else, Kelly found herself smiling as the two of them went on.

"So what do you two have planned for today?" asked Mrs. Pesca.

"Well, I thought we'd go to the steam vents," answered Jack quickly, "or the quarry cliff and maybe the algae ponds. And maybe we'll go for a swim or out in a boat. There's a group going to the reef later."

Though Kelly thought she'd probably have to get in a boat to leave the island, she wasn't so crazy about the idea.

"You mentioned school yesterday," she said to Jack. "Do you have to go today?"

"We're on vacation right now," he answered. "We go to school for three months at a time and then get a month off. We don't go back for about another week."

Jack's mother took their dishes and told her son not to overdo it, as Kelly was still recovering. She also reminded him not to forget his chores and to be careful.

"*Okay,* Mom," he moaned, rolling his eyes.

Jack and Kelly helped clear the table and wash the dishes. Jack showed Kelly the special stream where all the wastes from the house went. He explained that it flowed under the village to a wetland where the plants and soil filtered out all the things that could harm fish or other sea life when the water eventually went into the ocean.

"Help yourself to lunch whenever you want," said Mrs. Pesca. "Be back by dinner, and Jack, show Kelly where the sun cream is. She'll need it."

~   ~   ~

Before they left the house, Jack handed Kelly a coconut shell full of slimy white cream. He explained that it contained a chemical from an algae that lives in very shallow water on the coral reef. On the reef, the chemical protects the algae from getting fried by the strong tropical sun. The cream would prevent her skin from getting sunburned. On the island only babies and newcomers had to wear it, because as the native islanders got older their skin got darker and immune to sunburns.

"Is that why your skin is sort of shiny compared to mine?" asked Kelly.

"Yeah, our skin is definitely better," said Jack arrogantly, holding his arm next to hers.

Kelly looked a bit hurt.

"I mean it's…it's different, good for being in the sun and water," he said quickly. "Sorry, sometimes things just pop out of my mouth. Mom's always saying I should think before I speak."

Kelly was a bit surprised by Jack's apology.

"It's okay. When I spend too much time in the pool, my skin gets pruned—all wrinkled and white. I guess it really isn't the greatest for being in the water a lot."

"That doesn't happen to us. C'mon, put some of this stuff on and let's go."

Kelly smeared the cream over her arms, legs, and face. It was kind of stinky, but Jack assured her the smell would wear off as soon as she got in the sun. He helped put some of it on her back.

"Are there other people like me living here?" questioned Kelly.

Jack hesitated.

"Just a couple. C'mon, let's go."

9

Before they set out to explore the island, Jack had a few chores to do. Kelly joined him in the garden to help weed and gather ripe fruits and vegetables. As she knelt down to pick a plump red tomato, out of the corner of her eye she saw something large move nearby. Kelly froze.

"Ahh, Jack, there's a huge l…lizard over here," she whispered, "and it's looking at me like it's kinda hungry."

"That's no lizard. Its just Fred, our iguana," laughed Jack.

"Your iguana?"

"Yeah, watch this," he said, plucking a red flower from a nearby bush and holding it out to the large reptile. The iguana took a step toward him, bent its head down to his hand, and sucked the bloom up like a vacuum cleaner.

"Is that all Fred eats?" asked Kelly hopefully.

"Flowers, leaves, and some fruits…that's about it. Here try it."

Jack plucked another flower and handed it to her. Kelly took the bloom and eyed the iguana warily, thinking it looked a lot like a miniature dinosaur. It had leathery brown skin that was wrinkled and peeling, a long tapered tail, short thick legs with clawed toes, and dark beady eyes.

"C'mon, he won't bite you," assured Jack, gently taking her hand and lowering it toward Fred's mouth. Kelly stood rigidly, holding her breath. Just as before, the iguana bent its head down and sucked up the flower.

Kelly sighed in relief and smiled.

"Fred's great, though Mom hates it when he gets inside the house. Mostly he just hangs out in the garden."

"Are there a lot of iguanas around here, along with the land crabs?"

"They're around, though you don't see them too often, except at iguana beach…there are tons of them there. Some even swim. You want to go there?" asked Jack.

"I think I'll pass on iguana beach for now."

"Well, we could go to the steam vents. How about the algae ponds or the tortoise and goat farm or maybe the quarry cliff? A group is going out to the reef this afternoon. We should definitely go with them."

"How about the tortoise farm?"

Kelly had never seen a tortoise and that sounded pretty safe. No reason to push the brave thing too fast.

"We can go there and the steam vents. They're in the same direction. Let's see if Paroe and her brother, Skip, want to come. Their house is that one over there," said Jack, pointing toward a large stone house in the distance.

The home was bigger than the Pescas' and had two trees sprouting from its roof. There were small wooden bridges connecting various parts of the house. In front was an enormous fountain with three jumping stone dolphins at its center.

"That's some house," said Kelly as they walked toward it.

"Yeah, not really the biggest, but their father is the best stone builder on the island," said Jack. "Only problem is coconuts keep falling off and landing on the roof."

He pointed to a grove of tall, skinny coconut palms right next to the house. Several of the trees were bent at their base and leaned over the roof.

"One day a coconut fell onto the roof, rolled off, and hit Skip smack on the nose. There was blood everywhere."

"Was he okay?"

"Yeah, but it was really messy."

As they got closer to the house, Kelly repeatedly looked up, wary of falling coconuts.

They walked around the dolphin fountain; water was spouting through round holes atop all three of the stone creatures. The sculpture was sitting in a wide stream that flowed from underneath the house and wound its way through the yard. To get to the front door, they had to pass over an arched wooden bridge that crossed over the stream.

"Skip, Paroe, are you here?" asked Jack, leaning in through the open door.

Soon they heard footsteps and a tall, thin boy appeared.

"Hey, Jack, what's up?"

He too had red-brown hair, though his was shoulder-length and wavy. Several strands fell into his face and he flicked his head back so he could see. He had a narrow face and a noticeable bump in his nose just below his eyes, which were wide and slightly slanted at the corners. He wore an orange wrap decorated with white rays.

"Hey, Skip, this is Kelly," said Jack. "She's the one that washed up on the beach the other night. Skip's dad was the one that carried you to my house. We're going up to the tortoise farm and steam vents. You and Paroe want to come?"

"I don't know," groaned Skip, flipping back his wayward hair again. "Dad's out at the reef cliff getting rock for a new house. We're supposed to work on the garden. But look at it—man, what a disaster."

Paroe came to the door. Her hair was in a high ponytail again and she too was wearing an orange-colored wrap. Hers was decorated with sea turtles instead of rays.

"It wouldn't be such a mess if you'd water it every once in awhile," she said, punching her older brother in the arm.

"Hey, don't give me any trouble, pipsqueak. I'm in no mood for it today," replied Skip sourly.

"You're always in a bad mood," said Paroe, shaking her head and turning toward Kelly. "We used to have a great garden. Lucky our neighbor's is overflowing and they give us the extra." She pointed toward a house across the sandy walkway. A huge garden surrounded the small home; it was filled with an incredible assortment of fruit trees and vegetable plants.

Paroe wanted to go with Jack and Kelly, and Skip begrudgingly agreed to join them as well, lamenting that there wasn't anything else he could do to help the garden anyway. The two of them went into the house to do a few things before leaving.

"Ever since their parents split up," whispered Jack to Kelly, "the garden's been taken over by weeds and Skip's been really mad."

"Did they get divorced?" asked Kelly.

"Like you, about a year ago, this guy named Hank came to the island," said Jack in a soft voice, speaking fast. "He was flying a small plane and got caught in a wicked storm. Crashed up on the mountain." Jack pointed up toward the center of the island where a high rocky peak rose above the thick green vegetation along its sides.

"He stumbled down to the village in really bad shape. Their mother's a doctor, the one that checked you out yesterday, and while nursing him back to health, they sort of, well, got together."

"That must be really hard on Skip and Paroe," said Kelly sympathetically. "I can't imagine my parents not being together."

"Yeah, they've had a really hard time. Hank and their mother have a place outside the village. She comes down to see them pretty often, but it's been really rough. Skip hates Hank."

Just then, Paroe and Skip came out of the house. Skip had a knife in a goatskin sheath strapped to his waist. The four of them headed out through the village. Kelly thought it might be worth meeting this

Hank person since he didn't really belong on the island either. Maybe he wanted to go home too.

10

Jack, Kelly, Paroe, and Skip walked north, parallel to shore. As usual, Jack kept up a running dialogue, speaking rapidly and pointing out different family homes, where friends lived, and a large open building with stone benches set in a semicircle that was the village council hall. He explained that the village council made a lot of the decisions on the island, such as who could fish and how much they could take, and where they built new houses.

"See that path?" continued Jack. "It heads down to the pools that we were at yesterday, and that trail over there, it goes further north to the quarry cliffs. But we're going over here."

Jack turned onto a sandy path heading inland. Kelly followed, thinking it was strange that none of them asked her about her home and what it was like. Maybe it had something to do with this Hank guy.

Soon they left the stone homes of the village behind. In front of them, the land began to slope up toward the mountain at the island's center. A jungle of plants lined the path. Ferns taller than Kelly and vines thick as snakes hung over the trail. There were also wide trees with smooth brown trunks and roots that rose from the ground and merged with the branches above.

"Are there any snakes on this island?" asked Kelly, carefully watching where she stepped.

"Yeah, a couple, but they're not dangerous," responded Paroe. "They just eat frogs and stuff."

"Grrrreat," said Kelly sarcastically. For her, snakes were the land equivalent of sharks. She'd have to keep reminding herself that she was going to be brave from now on.

Up ahead to their left the jungle of plants gave way to a sloping grassy field. There were hundreds of brown lumps scattered across the grass.

"Here's the tortoise farm," announced Jack. "See all those brown things? Those are the tortoises."

Kelly followed as the other three jumped over a low stone wall and walked into the field.

"Are we supposed to be in here?" she asked.

"Sure, there's hardly ever anybody around," answered Jack quickly. "They're all at the egg-laying pens down the hill. Up here, it's just us and the tortoises. See, here's one."

The four of them came up to a huge tortoise—or maybe it was a turtle. Kelly wasn't really sure what the difference was. The animal was at least two feet high. It had a thick dark-brown shell that must have been two feet across as well. The wrinkly brown skin on its legs and neck looked like those of an elephant she'd once seen in a zoo. Its neck was long and its face was wrinkled with a short pointy nose. Kelly thought the tortoise looked really old and that its shell must be very heavy. The lumbering creature took two agonizingly slow steps, stopped, and pulled its neck and head in. Jack crouched down, leaning in near the head, and dramatically waved his hand dangerously close to the animal's mouth.

"They don't have any teeth, but they can still bite," he said, showing off. "They've got really strong jaws."

Just then, the tortoise extended its neck so that its mouth came perilously close to Jack's hand. Startled, he fell backward, landing with a thud on his butt.

"I hate it when they do that," said Jack, sheepishly.

Kelly, Skip, and Paroe couldn't help but laugh loudly as Jack turned red as a beet.

"Hey, you kids! What are you doing up there?" yelled a voice from the grassy slope below. "You're not supposed to be in here."

"Oops, must be feeding time. We'd better take off," shouted Jack as he ran back toward the stone wall. The others sprinted after him.

"I thought you said it was okay if we went in," huffed Kelly, out of breath from running and jumping the wall.

"The tortoise keepers don't really like people bothering them," said Skip, shrugging. "But we never harm 'em; it's not like we ride them or anything. Well, except for Angel. He got caught riding one once."

They crossed the path from the village, going down a trail in the opposite direction. Soon they came up to a sturdy wooden fence and another grassy field. As they approached the fence, three goats treaded over, their long ears flapping up and down.

"Lookin' for handouts as usual," laughed Paroe as she patted one on the head. "Sorry, forgot to bring treats this time." The goat searched her hand for food, like a horse looking for a carrot.

"Treats…they'll eat just about anything," snickered Skip as he broke off the top of a nearby plant and started to feed it to one of the goats.

Paroe reacted quickly, slapping her brother's hand away from the goat.

"*Skip,* don't you know that plant?" said Paroe. "It's *Dreamweed.* It'll make the goat sick. It'll put him to sleep or worse."

Kelly was surprised at how forceful Paroe sounded.

Jack explained that in school they had learned that the plant's leaves could be used to make a weak tea to help people sleep, and when the sap was put in a drink, it was like anesthesia.

"Oh, that little bit wouldn't have hurt it," said Skip.

Kelly looked over at Paroe. She was stroking one goat's neck, and the other two animals had come over and were nuzzling her arm.

"C'mon, let's go up the mountain to the steam vents. They're more exciting than these dumb animals," barked Skip.

"They're not dumb," countered Paroe calmly.

The goats seemed almost drawn to the girl.

Again Jack led the way as they headed back to the main path and further inland. The trail began to slope up more steeply and the vegetation thinned. Before long, Kelly saw scattered outcrops of dark, craggy rocks.

"It's not too much farther," announced Jack.

Kelly looked up ahead and saw mist rising from the mountainside. Then she heard the sound of running water. They walked around a sharp curve in the trail, and there ahead, sitting on a wide rock shelf carved into the mountainside, was a pool of blue-green water with a waterfall cascading into it. Huge green ferns and small flowering plants rimmed the pool's edges, and a thick mist rose from its surface over the waterfall.

"Isn't it pretty?" said Paroe.

Kelly nodded, staring at the beautiful view before her eyes.

Jack ran ahead to the water's edge and dipped his foot in.

"Just come and feel it, Kelly," he said.

Kelly followed and put her toes in. The water was as warm as a hot bath.

"Let's go up," said Skip as he nimbly climbed up the rocks next to the waterfall. Jack quickly followed.

Paroe hung back with Kelly.

"Don't worry, it's easy…there's stairs," she whispered.

Kelly thought it looked dangerous. But when she got up close, she saw that indeed there were crude steps chiseled into the cliff's face. She followed Paroe up the steps as spray from the waterfall soaked her hair and wrap. She was glad that Paroe had stayed behind and was with her as they went up.

"Up here," called Jack. He was with Skip further up the cliff where the stairs made a sharp left away from the waterfall.

Kelly and Paroe reached the other two, who were standing next to a deep crack in the black rock. Steam rose from the fissure and the surrounding rocks glistened with moisture.

"This is one of the steam vents," explained Jack. "The water comes down from the mountain. Well, really it's a volcano. You did know it's a volcano?"

Before Kelly could answer, he went on.

"The water heats up underground and flows through these cracks to the waterfall. By the time the water gets into the pool, it's cooled down. Want to go in?"

Kelly looked up at the rocky peak looming overhead.

"A volcano?" she said. "Has it ever erupted?"

"Stories are that it did a really long time ago. The only thing we've ever seen, or more like felt, is just a few earthquakes," answered Jack matter-of-factly, as if earthquakes and volcanoes were pretty standard stuff.

Kelly's eyes grew wide at the mention of earthquakes, another thing she'd always been scared of.

"It's just a little shaking," assured Jack. "My mom says the volcano is why our gardens grow so well, something about ash in the soil. Let's go in the pool."

Once again, Jack and Skip took off, heading down the stairs to the waterfall pool. Kelly and Paroe followed, making their way more carefully down the cliff. By the time the two girls got to the edge of the pool, the boys were already in the water floating on their backs.

While Paroe slipped into the water, Kelly stood at its edge. It looked pretty safe, but she couldn't see the bottom and that made her nervous.

"Don't worry," said Paroe, standing up. "It's shallow and there's nothing icky on the bottom, just rock."

Kelly sat down, swung her legs into the warm water, and carefully slipped in. It felt wonderfully warm and relaxing. The two-piece wrap she had on seemed to tighten just a little, feeling like a swimsuit in the water.

Kelly thought it looked strange as the four of them sat in the blue-green pool with just their heads out of the water and steam rising all around.

Paroe glanced at her brother, who was deep in conversation with Jack.

"What's it like where you come from?" she whispered to Kelly.

"You're the first person that's asked me that."

"Oh, I'm sorry," replied Paroe quickly. "You don't have to tell me."

"No, that's okay. It's just weird that nobody's asked me, that's all."

Paroe again glanced over at Skip and Jack.

"That's because my dad told us not to talk to you about it. Since you're going to have to stay here, he thought you'd get upset."

"I don't plan to stay here forever," responded Kelly without thinking. "I'm going to find a way to go home."

The boys must have overheard.

"Kelly, there's no way off the island," said Jack sternly. "The coral reef completely surrounds the island and no one's ever made it across."

"Well, then, how did I get here?" said Kelly more strongly. "There must be a way through the reef. When the dolphin pulled me here, I didn't see a reef or get hurt. And besides, Jack, your mom said some people disappeared. How do you know they didn't make it?"

"A dolphin brought you here?" inquired Paroe, her eyes wide in delight.

Kelly thought back to the night she arrived.

"I think so," she said, feeling the bruise where she had hit her head. "I fell off our boat in a storm. It was really bad. When it turned dark, I saw a glowing dolphin and it brought me here."

Unlike Kelly, they didn't seem the least bit surprised that a dolphin had helped her or that it was glowing. They explained that the glow was from algae in the ocean that produce light; in school they learned it was called bioluminescence.

"Where I come from, dolphins don't usually help people," noted Kelly, shaking her head. "In fact, people there do things that can hurt or kill dolphins."

"That's awful," said Paroe sadly. "No wonder they don't help you. Why do you want to go back to a place like that?"

"My family and friends are there and there's lots of cool stuff like cars and computers. Besides it's my home. It's where I live."

"From what I've heard there's lots of bad stuff there, like murders and pollution," said Skip scornfully.

Paroe climbed out of the pool and looked back at Skip.

"You know dad only tells us about the bad stuff because of Hank," she said. "There must be some good things too."

Paroe wasn't watching where she stepped and stumbled on a loose rock at the water's edge. Fortunately she didn't fall, but when she glanced down at her feet Paroe gasped loudly and then screamed for her brother.

In an instant he was at her side.

"What's the matter?" questioned Skip.

"*A bunch of centipedes,*" she answered, pointing to the ground. "*By my foot. Do something, Skip, they're gonna bite, hurry!*"

At her feet were several of the ugliest, squirmiest things Kelly had ever seen. They looked like a cross between a snake, a cockroach, and a spider—with more legs than the last two put together. There were at least three of the wriggling creatures and they were crawling over and around Paroe's foot.

"Don't move, Paroe," said Skip calmly. "Stay very still."

"What are they?" asked Kelly, climbing cautiously out of the pool.

Jack was quickly standing beside her.

"They're centipedes," he said, pointing to Paroe's foot. "Terrible creatures with a really nasty bite. See, they've got like a hundred legs and big pincers at the head."

Paroe was shaking.

"Come on, hurry up, Skip," she urged. "Do something. I know they're going to bite me."

"Just be still and I'll get them off," said Skip, taking his knife out of its sheath.

"*Just hurry.*"

Using the tip of the knife, Skip was able to flick two of the centipedes away.

"That's two of them, just one more," he said.

Unfortunately for Paroe, by now the last centipede was quite angry, and before Skip could get to it, the long, leggy, wriggling creature dug its sharp pincers deep into her bare foot.

Skip caught Paroe as she cried out and wheeled backward, nearly falling into the waterfall pool. The spot where the centipede had bitten was turning deep red and her entire foot was beginning to swell.

Skip picked up his younger sister.

"We'd better get her back to the village," he said with concern.

"No, take me to Mom," sobbed Paroe. "She's on the way; she's the best doctor. I want to go to Mom."

Kelly could tell that Skip wasn't happy about his sister's request, but he reluctantly agreed. She and Jack followed him at a jog as he quickly carried Paroe down the mountainside, backtracking the way they had come. Just past the tortoise and goat pens, but before they reached the village, Skip took a narrow trail leading off the main path. Soon they came to a small clearing. Skip stopped and looked up.

"Mom, are you home?" he shouted. "Mom, are you up there? Paroe's been bitten by a centipede."

Kelly looked up. This house was not built around a tree; it was actually constructed in the trees. It was made of wood and vines and sat about ten feet up off the ground.

The same small, slender woman who had checked Kelly out when she first landed on the island came out of the house to a wooden railing.

"Skip, is that you?" she asked. "What are you doing here? Is that Paroe? What's happened?"

Skip explained as the woman walked down a ramp to them.

She looked at Paroe's foot and felt her forehead.

"No fever yet. Let's get her inside."

Jack and Kelly followed as Skip carried Paroe up into the house in the trees.

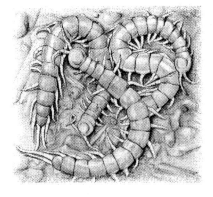

11

The first thing Kelly noticed when they entered the treehouse was the clutter. There were baskets and shells everywhere. She couldn't see inside most of them, though peeking out of the top of one basket were some plant leaves, and from another, a few pieces of tree bark. She looked inside a large clamshell as they passed; it contained a gray, slimy liquid-like substance. They were walking over a thick woven mat that sat atop floorboards of wood. The roof was made of dried palm fronds and the walls had been constructed from small tree trunks that were somehow stuck together.

Kelly followed as they entered a bedroom at the far end of the house. Skip laid Paroe carefully down on the bed; she was sweating profusely and her foot had swollen to the size of an inflated balloon.

Jack stood next to Kelly, unusually quiet.

"Is Paroe going to be okay?" she whispered.

Jack shrugged.

Paroe's mother came into the room stirring the contents of a small bowl.

"You did a great job getting her here quickly," she said. "Everyone reacts differently to stings and bites. Unfortunately, Paroe tends to react badly. Hopefully, this medicine will do the trick. Why don't you all go out and have a seat for a minute and I'll be right out."

Kelly, Jack, and Skip went out into the main room of the treehouse. As they were sitting down, a man walked in.

"Well, this is a nice surprise. Hello, Skip, Jack, so nice to see you."

"This isn't a social call," replied Skip curtly. "Paroe was bitten by a centipede."

"Is she all right?"

"Don't know…Mom's in with her now. Lucky we were nearby, since you're way out here."

"C'mon, Skip, we're not that far away and you know why we're here."

"Yeah, yeah, whatever," he muttered, looking at the floor.

Kelly thought the man looked older than her father. He had very short, silver-white hair and his face was well weathered, as if he'd spent a lot of time in the sun and wind. He had dark-blue eyes that weren't cloudy and a slightly crooked nose.

"Hello, you must be Kelly, the little girl everyone is talking about," he said. "My name is Hank Tenamaker. Just call me Hank. I came here about a year ago sort of like you, except that I crashed in my plane. Lucky for me Skip's mom was able to patch me up. She's a super doctor."

"Hi," replied Kelly. There were so many questions she wanted to ask him, but with everyone around waiting to hear about Paroe, she didn't think it was the right time.

Skip glared at Hank for a few minutes and then jumped up.

"I'm gonna check in with Mom and then head back to the village to let Dad know what's happened," he grumbled.

A few moments later, Skip came out of the bedroom looking relieved.

"Mom says she's gonna be okay. I'm out-a-here."

"Hold on, Skip," said Jack, jumping up. "I'll come with you."

Kelly didn't want to go, but she thought it would be weird if she remained behind. She stared at Hank, wishing that she could stay and talk with him.

"I'd better go too," she said.

"Why don't you come back tomorrow and visit Paroe. She'll probably need to stay here for a few days to rest," said Hank, almost as if he knew what Kelly was thinking.

"Okay, I'd like that. I really hope she's all right."

"See you tomorrow then, and don't worry, Paroe will be fine."

Kelly and Jack had to run to catch up with Skip, who was striding furiously down the path, mumbling to himself.

"He's not really that bad of a guy, Skip," said Jack. "C'mon, calm down."

"Not that bad of a guy? *Right!*" retorted Skip, glaring at Jack. "Easy for you to say. He didn't split up your folks."

"Well, at least Paroe's going to be okay," replied Jack.

"Yeah, just wait till my dad hears that she's at their place. He'll throw a fit," responded Skip, flicking his hair back and looking glumly down at his feet.

When they got to the outskirts of the village, Jack nudged Kelly in the direction of his house.

"Hey Skip, we're gonna head home," he said. "We're going out to the reef after lunch if you want to come."

"Nah, I'm gonna find my dad."

Kelly and Jack said good-bye and set off for the Pescas' house.

"Are there a lot of those centipede things around here?" asked Kelly, looking suspiciously at the path and where she was stepping.

"Not really," answered Jack. "You just have to keep an eye out. They like to hang out under rocks."

"I really hope Paroe's okay. She's been really nice."

"Yeah, everyone likes Paroe, especially the animals. Well, all but the centipedes, I guess."

"I have an older brother back home. His name's Thomas. I don't think he'd do for me what Skip did for Paroe. He mostly just teases me," noted Kelly sadly.

"You're lucky. I don't have any brothers or sisters. Always wished I did. If I was your older brother, I'd have helped you."

Kelly was a bit surprised. It was a very nice thing for Jack to say and slightly out of character. She smiled.

Before long, they were at the Pescas' small stone house.

Jack told Kelly that his mother was probably at one of the growing pools or out fishing.

"She and Dad are both great spearfishers. One day I want to be as good as they are. Let's grab a bite to eat and then see who's going to the reef."

Kelly's head was spinning. She'd been thinking of her family back home and Paroe's encounter with the awful centipedes. It had been sort of lucky, though, because she'd gotten to meet Hank. She wondered what her parents and brother were doing. Had they already forgotten about her and stopped looking?

She swore she wouldn't cry. She was done with that. She'd have lunch with Jack and then go out to the reef. Well, she'd have to play that one by ear. Sharks hang out on reefs, at least that's what all the television shows said. She wasn't sure that she was that brave just yet. At least tomorrow she could talk to Hank again. Maybe, just maybe, he had a family back home and wanted to leave the island also.

12

After lunch Jack and Kelly headed to the beach. When they arrived, there was a small group of kids milling about next to two large wooden canoes, both painted red.

"C'mon, this'll be fun," said Jack as he headed toward the group.

Kelly followed, hanging back a bit. She felt very self-conscious. When they had walked through the village, it seemed like everyone had been staring at her. She didn't have shiny, mocha skin, webbed hands and feet, or cloudy eyes that could see underwater.

Jack ran into the group and was immediately part of the conversation.

"Hey guys, this is Kelly. She's gonna come to the reef."

A boy about her brother's age stepped forward. He had small, squinty eyes and a sharp, angular nose and chin. His short hair and skin were a shade lighter than those of the other kids. With his hands on his hips, he looked Kelly over from head to toe.

"So this is the mermaid that washed ashore," he noted arrogantly. "Where's your tail, mermaid?"

A girl about the same age pushed him aside.

"Shut up, Angel," she said. "Hey Kelly. I'm Trig. Don't pay any attention to him."

She looked a bit like the boy, Angel—the same hair, though longer—but her eyes were larger, and when she smiled, dimples creased her cheeks.

"I'm sorry to say we're twins. Me and Angel, that is," said Trig, shaking her head.

"You're the lucky one, sis. Where would you be without me?" boasted her twin, prancing about.

Trig groaned and rolled her eyes skyward.

The next few minutes were spent with everyone introducing themselves. In addition to the twins, there was a short, pudgy boy named Hamlet—nicknamed Ham—a girl with wild hair like Jack's called Lizzy, and Sarg, a quiet, serious-looking boy.

None of them asked Kelly how she had gotten to the island, where she was from, or what it was like. Again she thought it was very odd. They did, however, take her over to the canoes and explain how they were built on the island. As usual, Jack did most of the talking.

"In school we learn a lot about the ocean," he began, "what lives there and how to farm algae. We also learn how to dive on the reef and build boats. See, they each have paddles to row, or if there's wind, we can put up a sail. And—"

"Okay, enough already," interrupted Angel. "Are we gonna talk all day or go to the reef? Split up and get in a boat."

"You and Jack come with me," said Trig, taking Kelly's arm and steering her to one of the canoes nearby.

Kelly wasn't so sure about going out to the reef, but she definitely felt more comfortable going with Trig and Jack than with Angel. Sarg, Ham, and Lizzy went with Angel in the other boat.

"You can sit on the middle seat," said Trig, seeming to sense Kelly's unease. "Jack and I will take the ones at the bow and stern. There are only two paddles, so you won't have to do a thing."

Jack and Trig pushed the canoe down to the water's edge. They helped Kelly climb in and sit on a narrow bench midway down the length of the boat. A small mast and a boom with a sail wrapped around it were tied down next to where she sat. They pushed the boat into the water and jumped in. The boat rolled slightly. Kelly tensed and held on to the sides of the canoe.

"Be brave," she whispered to herself.

Jack and Trig each grabbed a paddle from the canoe's floor and started stroking, pushing the boat seaward. Kelly held on and tried to breathe, but it felt as if she just wasn't getting enough air.

"It'll be better once we get going," said Trig.

And sure enough, as soon as the boat was moving through the bright blue water, they barely rolled at all. Both Trig and Jack seemed completely at ease paddling. Kelly took a deep breath, trying to relax, and looked into the water. It was so clear she could see the white, sandy bottom moving past. A few moments later, patches of green seagrass went by and then a few small brown coral heads. She even thought she saw a school of fish swim lazily under the boat.

"Hey Jack, let's start at a small patch reef before going all the way out," suggested Trig.

"Okay," he replied, steering the canoe toward a dark spot ahead.

As they got closer, Angel's canoe caught up with them, nearly ramming them from behind.

"Why are you guys stopping here?" he barked. "C'mon, let's go out farther to the real reef."

"We'll meet you out there, Angel," answered Trig. "We're gonna stop here for a few minutes."

"Wimps!" yelled Angel. He splashed them with his paddle and headed the other canoe seaward toward the main reef, the one that encircled Dolphin Island.

Jack grabbed a line attached to the boat's bow.

"I'll be right back," he said, and before Kelly could even blink, Jack dove off the boat. A minute later he popped up next to the canoe.

"That should hold us. I tied off to some dead coral."

Kelly was shaking. They definitely expected her to go in the water.

"Uhh, you can swim, can't you?" questioned Trig.

"Yeah, I can swim," answered Kelly. "I'm just a little nervous since the storm."

She didn't mention her fear of sharks or just about everything else living in the ocean.

Trig took her time getting in.

"It's really safe here," she said. "Most of the time, waves break on the reef farther out, so it's calm back here in the lagoon. Watch, you just swing your legs over the side like this and slip in—nothing to it."

Kelly watched as Trig slid into the water. She and Jack looked so comfortable in the sea. With their webbed hands and feet, they moved through the water seemingly without effort.

Jack appeared beside the boat again.

"Hey, you should see it down here," he said enthusiastically. "There's a queen triggerfish and a pair of banded butterflyfish, and I just saw a *Tripneustes* sea urchin...they look like furry white muffins. C'mon, Kelly, give it a try. It's great."

Both Jack and Trig made it look so easy that Kelly wanted to go in. She wanted to see what they were seeing and feel as comfortable as they did. She swung her legs over the side just like Trig had demonstrated and sat there for a few minutes peering into the water—nothing came up to bite her feet, which were now dangling in the sea. She held tightly onto the side with shaking hands. Then, with great resolve, she took a deep breath, closed her eyes, and slid into the ocean.

The water felt cool and refreshing. It was also flat calm, nothing like during the storm. Trig came up beside her.

"See, the water's great," she said reassuringly. "Come look at this triggerfish. It's really beautiful, and by the way, it's the fish I'm named after."

The water was only about ten feet deep. Trig dove gracefully beneath the surface pointing to something below. Kelly followed, but when she opened her eyes, they stung from the saltwater and everything looked blurry. She couldn't make out what Trig was trying to show her.

Kelly went back to the surface. She felt so awkward and clumsy compared to Jack and Trig. They were swimming around as if they were fish themselves—going down and pointing to things, then coming up to the surface to tell Kelly what they were.

"See that mustard-colored mound? That's a coral…and look at the one over there—looks like fuzzy tan pillars."

Kelly desperately wanted to see what they were showing her, but her eyes were tearing and everything underwater looked so blurry. She could sort of tell the outline of a coral or the shape of a fish, but she couldn't see anything in detail. She grabbed onto the side of the canoe. After a few minutes she let go, swam a little bit, and then came back.

Jack swam over to see how Kelly was doing. He then showed her how to get into the boat by pulling herself up on the side and swinging her legs over. With his webbed feet, it was easy for Jack to get back in. One strong kick with his flipper-like feet and he was propelled up onto the boat's edge. Kelly, however, had a much harder time. After several unsuccessful and awkward attempts, Jack helped by pulling her in.

Trig jumped in quite easily.

"Oh, don't worry," she chuckled. "It took me forever to learn how to get back in."

"Yeah and you should see Ham," added Jack. "He still can't get in without help."

Kelly rubbed her eyes.

"So what'd ya think?" asked Jack.

"I think it would be better if I had my goggles."

"Oh yeah, I forgot, your eyes aren't like ours. Could you see anything?"

"Kinda, I guess."

Trig looked over the side of the canoe.

"You know, it's so calm and clear today," she observed. "You can almost see everything right from the boat."

Amazingly enough, as Kelly looked over the side, she realized that Trig was right. She could see the yellowy mustard coral and the ones that looked like fuzzy tan pillars. She could actually see them better from the boat than in the water. She saw the pretty light-blue triggerfish with its wispy fluttering fins and a pair of small, yellow, round fish with vertical black bands, like racing stripes, running down their bodies. And there was the muffin-like sea urchin that was covered with so many short, white spines it looked furry.

"Hey, what's that big blue fish right there?" asked Kelly, pointing to a large turquoise-colored fish as it swam beneath the canoe.

"Oh, that's a parrotfish," answered Jack, looking over the side. "There are tons of them around here. They've got really big front teeth."

"*Big teeth?*" questioned Kelly, looking fearfully into the water.

"Big buckteeth to scrape algae off the reef," said Jack, smirking. "They're grazers, harmless, kind of like underwater goats. And at night, it's really cool, for protection they sleep in holes and spin a web of poisonous slime around themselves. Paroe is named after the parrotfish, although she doesn't do the web thing, of course."

"Are you all named after fish?" asked Kelly.

"Yeah, mostly fish," answered Jack. "Have you ever heard of an amberjack or a skipjack?"

"Nope," said Kelly.

"Well, now you know the real Jack," he declared, puffing out his chest.

Trig chuckled, shook her head, and looked at Kelly.

"Do you still want to go to the reef farther out?"

"Okay, but I may stay in the boat. There are sharks out there, right?"

Kelly half-expected Jack to go into a speech about how he had swum with "tons" of them.

"Really, you don't need to worry about them," said Jack. "There are sharks, but mostly they stay on the other side of the reef. In the lagoon we sometimes see nurse sharks and a few small lemons or blacktips.

The nurse sharks sleep on the bottom and are pretty friendly. They eat mostly crabs and other stuff from the seafloor. The lemons and black-tips are pretty skittish; they almost always take off as soon as they see you. And besides, like I said, I've been in the water with lots of them."

"They're really not a problem," added Trig, shaking her head good-naturedly.

"I may just stay in the boat anyway," said Kelly, still hesitant.

"That's cool," said Trig.

Jack jumped in and quickly untied the canoe. Then he and Trig paddled seaward, heading them toward the other boat and the coral reef that encircled Dolphin Island. As they got farther out in the lagoon, the water turned a darker shade of blue. It was still only about fifteen feet deep. Kelly watched as they passed over other patch reefs. She saw the yellow-brown color of coral pass by. Some were shaped just like the small round rocks that lined the village's walkways, while others branched out like miniature trees. She also saw large dark-purple sea fans waving slowly back and forth as if in a light breeze.

"Wow, what's that?" asked Kelly, pointing to a large creature passing beneath the canoe.

"That's an eagle ray," replied Jack. "Its color gives it away, purple on top with white spots."

Just then, a sea turtle poked its head out of the water in front of the boat. As soon as it saw them, the shy creature tucked its head in and dove for the bottom. With the water so calm and so much to see, Kelly had nearly forgotten her fears of the sea.

As they got closer to the reef, the water began to get shallower. Soon they were gliding in next to the other canoe. It was tied off about twenty feet behind the reef in just six feet of water.

Jack went into his fast-talking tour guide mode.

"See how it gets shallow behind the reef? This is the back reef. The other side drops off fast and gets much deeper; that's the fore reef. At its very top, the shallowest part, is the reef crest. See the coral on the back reef—look at the one over there, looks like a rolling field of purple fingers, and see the one over there like a tangle of skinny branches…"

Before Jack could go on, a hand followed by a wet, pudgy head popped up beside Kelly, startling her.

"Hey, you guys made it," said Ham with a smile.

Jack dove in, tied the boat off beside the other canoe, and came up next to Ham.

"Where are the others?" he asked.

"They're just over there," replied Ham, pointing down the reef a bit. "There's a nurse shark sleeping under a coral head and Angel's trying to get in and pull its tail."

"Ugh, what an idiot," said Trig, shaking her head. "He's definitely going to get bitten one of these days."

Kelly looked questioningly at Trig.

"They don't normally bite," said Trig, sighing with disgust. "Unless of course you do something stupid like pull their tail. I'll be right back."

She jumped into the water and swam over to where the others were circling a large coral head. Kelly assumed she was going to try to talk her twin out of playing cat and mouse with the shark. Ham followed.

"Want to go see the shark?" asked Jack.

"No thanks," answered Kelly quickly. "I think I'll just sit here for a little bit."

"You okay?"

"Yeah, I just need a minute, that's all."

Jack swam after the others and Kelly looked around. She thought she'd be scared, sitting all alone in a canoe far from shore. But surprisingly she felt fine. In fact, she felt better than fine. Three times now she'd been in the ocean—during the storm, with the rays, and then just a few minutes ago over the patch reef. Nothing had tried to attack her and it was a lot like swimming in a pool. Now she actually wanted to go in the ocean. She wanted to see more fish and the colorful corals. Kelly wished she had her goggles or even a mask. How things had changed. Just a week ago she would never have imagined feeling this way. She wasn't quite ready to see a shark, though.

Just then, the other kids came back to the boat. With a little coaxing from his sister, Angel had given up on teasing the shark.

"So are you coming in or what? Are you *scared?*" teased Angel, sounding a lot like Kelly's older brother, Thomas.

At first Kelly looked around tentatively. Then she smiled and simply slipped into the water. She swam over to where the sandy bottom sloped up onto the back reef; it was like the side of a small underwater hill. At the top of the slope, she was in just two feet of water. Corals were scattered about; some were small knobby heads and others formed little, branching thickets. Avoiding the coral, she found an open sandy spot, put her feet on the bottom, and stood up. On the reef behind her, there were small waves breaking, but next to her, the water was smooth as glass. To her sides the glassy water and reef extended for as far as she could see, curving in the distance around the island.

Kelly looked more closely at the reef. Just beneath the water's surface, small hills and ridges of coral created an incredible undersea landscape. In between the bright yellow, brown, and purple mounds of coral were narrow channels of sand, piles of rubble, and patches of colorful algae and sponge. In some places where the corals overlapped, it reminded her of a multicolored gingerbread house.

Standing there in the shallow, calm, clear water, Kelly could even see fish darting here and there. She turned toward the reef crest, put her face in the water, and opened her eyes. There was a huge school of small silver fish hovering over a wide mound of purple finger coral. She lifted her feet off the bottom and floated into the silvery school. In a graceful dance, the school parted as she floated in. As she moved, the school of fish moved. Kelly forgot about her eyes stinging or the nurse shark sleeping not so far away as the school of fish shimmered and danced before her eyes.

The other kids swam up to Kelly and the small fish scattered. For the next hour, they explored the back reef. Kelly floated at the surface and the others pointed out different creatures. Lizzy spotted a huge orange starfish. Sarg found a lobster with long skinny spines that waved toward her when she hovered just over it. And Ham showed her a large boxy cowfish with polka-dot skin, big eyes, and a small puckered-up mouth.

Later, back in the canoe, Kelly sat smiling. She loved the reef with its silvery schools of fish and brightly colored creatures. It was like an undersea city, with differently shaped buildings and a great assortment of residents. She wished that she too had cloudy eyes and webbed hands and feet.

As they were getting ready to leave, Angel came over and began to rock the canoe.

"Oh no! It's a storm. It's getting rough."

"Shut up, quit it," responded Trig. "You're such a pain."

Clearly Angel was trying to frighten Kelly.

"I'm *soooo* scared," said Kelly.

Angel looked up in surprise; this was not the reaction he had expected. Disappointed, he swam silently to the other canoe.

"Good one, Kelly," said Trig, smiling.

"Yeah, you showed him," added Jack.

The wind was blowing onshore, so they put the sails up and let it push the two boats back to the beach, paddling only to steer. It was smooth sailing all the way in, and they were quickly aground on the sand. Kelly helped as they all pulled and pushed the boats high up onto the beach.

While the others stowed the paddles and sails, talking about things going on in the village, Kelly looked out to sea. It looked different now. It wasn't scary or simply beautiful; now she wanted to see and to learn more. For her, there was a new magical world beneath the waves. She thought back to the dolphin that had brought her to the beach and to the island. She wondered if she would ever see it again or feel the dolphin's smooth skin while gliding beside it in the sea. Maybe it wouldn't be so bad if she had to stay on the island. But then she thought about her parents and her friends back home. No, she had to find a way off of Dolphin Island, a way to go home.

~   ~   ~

Kelly and Jack were walking back through the village. It was nearly sunset and starting to get dark. Up ahead on the sandy walkway, something darted across the sand. Jack sprinted after it.

"What is it?" Kelly yelled after him.

But Jack didn't answer. He was too busy chasing whatever it was. Then he dove headfirst into a big round bush. The entire shrub began to shake and shudder, and leaves flew into the air.

"Jack, are you okay? What is it?"

Then the bush suddenly became still and Jack emerged. He looked a mess with leaves and small twigs sticking out of his hair and scratches all over his body. He was examining a small gash on his thumb.

"What was it?" asked Kelly expectantly.

"Land crab, huge one," answered Jack, holding his hands nearly two feet apart, "and I almost had it."

Kelly chuckled. She didn't think it was really that big or that he had almost caught it.

"So Jack, what's with that Angel kid anyway?" she asked.

"You notice how his and Trig's hair and skin are a little lighter than mine?"

"Yeah," replied Kelly, nodding.

"Well, kinda like you, his father is an outsider. He was in a shipwreck or something years ago and came to live on the island. He married their mother and they had kids, Angel and Trig. I think Angel makes up for feeling different by being obnoxious, and he's always getting into trouble."

"Trig is so nice, though."

"Yeah, they're kinda opposites, I guess. When they were younger, kids made fun of them because it took them longer to get webs on their hands and feet, and they couldn't see as well underwater. Trig always took it pretty well, but Angel got into a lot of fights."

"Kids where I come from can be mean like that too," said Kelly, "especially with people who are different."

"I don't know," said Jack. "I always thought it would be kinda cool to be a little different, not the same as everybody else."

Kelly thought about that, given her current situation. Where she came from she always felt so average and so ignored. But here she was different and people were constantly staring at her. Almost everyone else had webbed feet and hands, cloudy eyes, and shiny skin. Now she sort of wished she were more average, more like everyone else on the island.

13

The following morning Kelly lay in bed thinking about the previous several days. She had hiked up to and floated in the waterfall pool. She had stood with stingrays and swum among the fish on a coral reef. She had survived the storm and flew through the sea at night beside a dolphin. For the first time in her life, she felt...*adventurous.* She thought—*if only Thomas or Dad could see me now.* She then thought about her parents; she missed them terribly. This morning she'd go see Hank and ask him if he wanted to leave also and if he knew of a way off the island.

Kelly joined Mr. and Mrs. Pesca at breakfast. Jack, as usual, was still asleep.

"I was thinking I'd go see Paroe this morning," she said, "and maybe talk with Hank."

"It would be nice to visit Paroe," said Mrs. Pesca, adding with concern, "but maybe you should stay away from that Mr. Tenamaker. He's a troublemaker."

"But he's like me, from somewhere else. He seemed pretty nice yesterday when I met him."

Mr. Pesca looked at his wife.

"Honey," he said, "it might be a good thing for her to chat with Hank. He's had to come to terms with living here as well."

"She could talk with Trig and Angel's father. He's adapted extremely well. But I suppose there's no harm in just talking. Okay, but it's probably best to wait for Jack so he can show you the way."

"That's all right, I think I can find it," responded Kelly quickly.

"Well, just be careful," said Mrs. Pesca, "and come back right after your visit so we know you found it all right."

With that, Kelly chugged down a glass of milk and left the table. She put on some of the stinky sunscreen and hurried off. She wanted to get out quickly and quietly, before Jack woke up and wanted to go with her. She liked Jack, but didn't think he would understand why she wanted to talk with Hank so badly or why she wanted to leave the island. When Kelly stepped out the door, she stumbled, nearly tripping over Fred, the iguana.

After recovering from her iguana surprise, Kelly headed north through the village the way they had gone the previous day. She passed quickly by the Aguans' house and continued on, looking for the correct trail leading inland. It wasn't like home with street signs and stoplights. There were a few main walkways with side trails leading off in different directions and they were all unmarked.

Ahead and to her left was a path leading toward the island's interior. She thought it was about the right distance from the Aguans' house. She turned onto it and headed inland. Just a short distance down the trail, it split into two. She didn't remember there being a fork yesterday when Jack had been leading, but then again she hadn't really been paying attention. Kelly decided to take the path on the left. If it didn't look right, she could always double back and take the other trail.

Like yesterday the path began to slope upward, and tropical plants grew lushly on both sides. After a while, Kelly saw an open field and realized it was the tortoise farm, except this time it was on her right instead of on her left like yesterday. The turnoff to the treehouse should have been before the farm. She must be on the wrong trail. But it was still early and Kelly was enjoying the walk in the morning's coolness. In her new spirit of adventure, she decided to explore just a little further before turning back.

The trail curved to the left and she went on. Large vines hung down and it got darker as the trail became more overgrown. Kelly thought about heading back. Then up ahead she saw something very strange. There was an odd blue glow coming from a wide hole in the side of a cliff. She decided to investigate.

The hole was lined with green moss and grass, and partially blocked by two small trees. She stepped around the trees and peered in. She couldn't see in very far, but it looked like the entrance to a cave. The opening was large enough for Kelly to fit through. She knew she shouldn't go in, but the blue light coming out of the cave was just so curious. She squeezed through.

From outside, the cave's walls had appeared black, but once inside she saw that they were actually creamy tan in color and very smooth. The floor was made of the same odd rock with scattered mounds that looked like enormous layer cakes covered in creamy tan frosting. Long pillars of the smooth stone hung down from the ceiling as well. Kelly began to weave her way in and around the strange structures in the cave. The floor was angled slightly downward and slippery, so she had to go slowly. The weird blue light seemed to be coming from farther down in the cave. If she just went a bit further, she thought she might see its source.

Kelly carefully lifted one foot around a knee-high, smooth mound. She then shifted her weight so that she could bring her other leg around as well. It was a mistake. Her right foot slipped on the slick rock and in an instant she was on her butt. With the angle of the cave's floor and its slipperiness, she started sliding—sliding downward toward the source of the eerie blue glow. She tried to stop, looking and reaching for something to grab onto. But the floor of the cave was just too slick. Kelly kept sliding.

The blue light was now getting brighter and the slope of the floor steeper. She began to slide faster. Kelly searched desperately for a way to stop. She tried kicking her heels into the rock, but it was too hard. She was still sliding, sliding downward toward the blue glow.

Moments later, just a few feet ahead, off to the right, she saw a cone-shaped rock sticking up. As Kelly started to slide by, she lunged, throwing both arms around the rock, hoping she could hang on. Her legs flew out beneath her and her stomach hit the cave's floor, but she kept her arms firmly around the rock. She lay still, breathing hard, thankful to have stopped. Then she carefully pulled herself up into a sitting position, wedged behind the cone-shaped rock.

Kelly looked back and could barely see the opening to the cave. But just below her, she could now make out the source of the glow. There was a pool of water at the cave's bottom emanating blue light. Pulses of blue-green occasionally flashed within the water. A little farther and she would have landed right in the glowing pool. Then she heard voices in the distance.

"Is there someone back there?" inquired a distant voice in a tone suggesting she shouldn't be there.

Kelly looked quickly back toward the opening and started climbing. She didn't want to be discovered in the cave and get into trouble. She tried to climb as quickly and as quietly as possible, but on the slippery rock it was difficult. Her legs began to ache and her arms burned with the effort. And with every step she was sure she'd slip and start sliding downward again.

"Is someone back there?" yelled the voice, a bit louder this time.

Kelly climbed faster. When she finally reached the cave's entrance, she leapt through and spilled out onto the grass. She lay there for several minutes catching her breath, enjoying the air and solid ground. Looking at the hole in the cliff, she wondered if it was part of the cave where they grew the glowing algae for the light orbs.

After a few more minutes of rest, Kelly walked, a bit shakily, back to where the trail had split. She took the other path, hoping it would lead to the treehouse. Soon there was a narrow trail to the right and she took it. The path opened up into a small clearing and there ahead stood the house in the trees.

She didn't want to shout, but she wasn't sure how else to let them know she was there. It wasn't as if there was a doorbell to ring. Kelly walked up the ramp past a small porch. In the doorway there was a fine mesh curtain waving in a gentle breeze.

Kelly knocked on the wooden door frame.

"Hello, is anyone home?" she asked tentatively.

Paroe's mother, Pearl, came to the door.

"Hi, is Paroe here? Is she okay?" asked Kelly.

"Come in, come in, she's doing just great," replied the woman. Kelly thought she seemed more relaxed and pleasant than before.

Paroe and Hank were sitting at a small table chatting.

"Hi Kelly," said Paroe, whose foot was wrapped in bandages and stretched out on a small chair.

"How are you?" inquired Kelly.

"Oh, I'm okay," replied Paroe, a bit embarrassed. "My foot's still pretty sore and I can't walk too well yet. But I feel much better."

"I'm glad you're okay. That thing that bit you was really awful."

"Oh, don't blame the centipedes," said Paroe. "It was my fault. I scared them when I tripped over the rock they were living under."

Kelly thought it was kind of a weird thing to say. She would have hated the creatures if they had bitten her.

"Just like our Paroe to be on the animal's side," said Hank, mussing her hair. "We're glad you came back to visit."

"Well, I...ahh...wanted to see how Paroe was doing and all."

Paroe's mother offered Kelly a seat with the others and asked if she'd like something to drink. Kelly requested a glass of water and sat next to Paroe.

The four of them chatted for a while. Kelly told them about the previous day's trip to the coral reef and Paroe tried to convince her that centipedes weren't really that bad.

"Even when Paroe was a baby, animals always seemed to like her," explained Paroe's mother. "Iguanas would come over and sit beside her.

Birds would land at her feet and eat out of her hand. Once we even found a pelican nestled next to her on the beach when she was taking a nap."

"Oh, Mom, you tell everyone that story," said Paroe, blushing.

"So Kelly, where exactly do you come from?" asked Hank.

Paroe looked at Kelly expectantly, while her mother leaned in a bit closer.

"I live in Massachusetts with my parents and older brother. We were on vacation sailing when a wave knocked me off the boat in a storm."

"I've visited Boston several times," noted Hank. "It was quite nice."

"Where are you from?" asked Kelly.

"Well, I travel a lot," he answered. "But I have a home in the mountains of Colorado. I was doing some business in the Bahamas and wanted a break. I fly a lot at home, so I decided to rent a plane and explore a little. Just my luck, lightning struck the plane in a bad squall and, well, here I am." Winking at Paroe's mother, he added, "Well, I was lucky in some ways."

Paroe's mother blushed.

Kelly wasn't sure how much to ask, especially in front of Paroe and her mother.

"Do you have a family in Colorado? Don't you miss them?"

"I'm divorced and my kids are all grown up," replied Hank. "But yes, I do miss them and the mountains back home."

Pearl then told them that Paroe needed to get some rest and ushered her, hopping, into the bedroom, assuring Kelly she'd be up and around soon.

Kelly watched as they left and then turned to Hank.

"Don't you want to go home?" she inquired quietly.

Hank sat back in his chair, thinking for a moment.

"After I crashed, Paroe's mother nursed me back to health," he said. "At first we were just friends, but with time I came to like her very much. And she felt the same way about me. But many of the people in the village are angry with me, and it's become hard on Pearl. Dolphin

Island is a very beautiful place, but truthfully it is not my home, and yes, I'd like to go back."

Kelly liked how Hank talked to her like an adult.

"I really miss my parents and want to go home, but they say there's no way off the island."

Hank stared at Kelly for a few minutes before speaking.

"From what I've heard, the few people that have tried to leave have either been badly hurt or have vanished," he said. "The way I figure it, or maybe hope, is that if they disappeared, they could have found their way to a passing ship or another island."

"Does that mean you're going to try to leave the island?"

At this point Paroe's mother came back and sat down, putting a finger to her lips indicating for them to be quiet.

"Back home I was an architect," explained Hank, lowering his voice. "I helped people design and build things. For the past several months I've been building a small boat in secret, specially designed to get over the reef. In just about a week, the tide will be one of the highest of the year and we plan to leave the island. Pearl and I."

"But what about Paroe and Skip?" asked Kelly.

Pearl looked very seriously at her.

"I love them both with all my heart," she said. "They have their father here who loves them and lots of friends. I'm not sure Skip or many of the others here will ever forgive me for leaving his father. I think it might be best if I leave with Hank."

Kelly didn't think she sounded very sure.

"Can I come with you?" she asked hopefully.

"It will be very dangerous," replied Hank. "I think it would be better for you to stay here."

"No, I have to go home," pleaded Kelly. "This is not where I belong. I mean, everyone's been great, except maybe Angel, but I should be with my parents. I can do it. I made it through the storm. Take me with you."

"I don't think so," said Hank kindly, looking at the young girl longing desperately to go home. "Well, I'll tell you what, how about we think about it. But whatever happens, you must not tell anyone about this, as they will surely try to stop us from going."

"I won't tell anyone, I swear," said Kelly. "Oh, please take me. I can help."

Just then, Kelly remembered the dolphin.

"A dolphin brought me through the reef the night I came to the island," she added enthusiastically. "There must be a safe way across."

Hank thought for a moment.

"Hmm…but how do we find this way across," he pondered. "We've looked and looked. No one on the island knows a safe way to get a boat through."

Kelly was trying not to cry. Hank smiled kindly.

"Look, Pearl and I will talk about it. You can come back tomorrow and we'll let you know."

Just then they heard someone calling from outside.

"Hey Kelly, are you up there? It's me, Jack. Is Paroe okay? Are you up there?"

Hank looked at Kelly.

"You'd better go now," he said. "We'll talk it over and see you tomorrow. Remember, not a word."

Jack said hello to Paroe, and then he and Kelly headed back to the village.

14

Kelly was going to spend the rest of the day with Jack exploring more of the island, yet she was distracted with thoughts of going home. She just had to convince Hank to take her. If only she knew how the dolphin had brought her through the reef.

They started the day's tour at the quarry cliff. The village builders were cutting huge blocks of white stone from the side of a hill. Jack pointed out different kinds of coral in the cliff and they talked about how they compared with what they had seen on the living reef.

Next they went to the algae ponds.

"See that reddish pond? That's where we grow red algae that are used for dye, to thicken paint, and for food," explained Jack. "And the green pond over there, that's where seaweed salad comes from. It can also be pressed together into a wrap for sandwiches."

"Sounds just yummy," Kelly said sarcastically.

At another of the ponds, people were chopping off the base of a golden-colored algae. It grew in very long strands that were speckled with clusters of small round balls.

"The balls have oil in them," continued Jack, "to help the algae float. We harvest them and use the oil for cooking and candles. The part attached to the rocks is boiled down to make really strong glue. And in that pond over there, we grow tiny crustaceans, called copepods, to feed the fish and other animals in the sea pools. Oh, and see that other pond nearby? That's the squid pool."

"Do you eat the squid?" asked Kelly, really hoping that's not what they'd be having for dinner that night.

"Sometimes, but mainly we harvest their ink to use in books and things."

"Where do you get the paper for books?"

"Oh, that's easy," said Jack. "We mash up dried coconut husks in water, press it into sheets, and then dry it. I'll show you some at home. Hey, let's go to the salt flat. It's a little bit of a walk, but on the way back we can stop at the pools and say hi to Sundy. He likes visitors and maybe the dolphins will be there."

At the word *dolphin*, Kelly quickly agreed. In truth she was still distracted. She kept thinking about Hank and Pearl and their plan to leave the island. She knew it would be dangerous, but she desperately wanted to go. If only she could figure out how the dolphin had brought her to the island.

It took them about half an hour to get to the salt flat; it was out past the sea pools to the north of the village. The salt flat was a wide sandy field encrusted with a layer of shiny crystals. It was radiant in the bright tropical sun and Kelly had to squint from the glare.

"See the low wall surrounding the flat and the small canal at the far end," explained Jack.

A narrow canal connected the salt flat to the ocean. At the moment, the water in the canal reached only up to the edge of the sand.

"As the tide rises," Jack went on, "the water flows in and over the salt flat. When there are a couple of inches of water over it, we close off the canal. After a few hours, if it's sunny, all of the seawater on the flat evaporates, leaving the salt behind. Then we sweep the salt crystals up off the surface."

They walked over to a three-foot-high pile of shiny, translucent crystals. Jack picked up a handful and passed it to Kelly.

"I never really thought about where salt comes from," noted Kelly. "Does it taste like salt?"

After she asked, Kelly realized it was a pretty stupid question and waited for Jack to say something or make fun of her.

Instead, Jack just put a shiny crystal flake in his mouth and gestured for Kelly to do the same.

"Yup, tastes like salt," said Kelly, laughing awkwardly. "What was I expecting, pepper?"

This time they both laughed.

"C'mon, let's go see Sundy," said Jack.

They left the salt flat and hiked to the sea pools along the shoreline. In some places it was easy going along a sandy beach; in other spots they had to scramble over jagged rocks or wade through the water. It was harder for Kelly than for Jack; her bare feet were far more sensitive, and she had to step carefully on and between the rocks.

"Watch out for sea urchins," warned Jack. "Especially the ones with long, black spines. They're tipped with poison."

Kelly looked into the water, taking even more care when placing her feet.

"I once saw a guy step on a bunch of those urchins," added Jack, shaking his head. "His foot looked awful and got huge. He had to be carried away."

"Thanks for telling me that," said Kelly. "I feel *sooo* much better now, walking barefoot and all."

"Don't worry, my mom told me what to do if you get stuck."

"Yeah?"

"Oh, you just pee on it," said Jack, smirking.

"Ugh, you're not peeing on me—that's *disgusting!*" exclaimed Kelly.

"Hey, you'd have to pee on yourself," laughed Jack. "I'm just telling you what you're supposed to do."

Coming around a bend in the island, they saw the sea pools ahead. Sundy was sitting in the shade of a nearby palm tree.

"Hi Sundy," they said, jogging over.

"Hey there, Jack and Miss Kelly. How are you this fine day?"

"Just showing Kelly around some more," answered Jack. "Thought we'd stop by to say hello."

"Well, hello then. You came by at just the right time. I'm doing a little repair work and could use a few more hands," said Sundy, holding up the edge of a large net. "Here, each of you grab a corner and help me spread this out so I can see where the rest of the holes are."

Jack and Kelly both took hold of the net and began walking backward. As Kelly shuffled back, she stopped momentarily, looking out at the ocean to see if there were any dolphins around. Jack didn't see her stop and continued walking, spreading the net out. At first the net bumped Kelly a bit as Jack kept going, and then it knocked her right off her feet and she fell backward onto the sand.

"Oops, sorry about that," said Jack. "Guess I just don't know my own strength." He then attempted to display the muscles in his skinny arms—if there had been muscles, that is.

Kelly and Sundy both looked at him and laughed. Kelly got up, brushing the sand off.

"Yeah Jack, you're such a hulk," she said good-naturedly.

Jack shrugged, smiled, and chuckled along with them.

"Okay, that's good," said Sundy after they had spread the net out a little further. "Set it down right there. It's nice to have a little help. Would you like some mango juice? My wife makes the best juice on the island, and every morning she gives me more than I can possibly drink."

Jack and Kelly gladly accepted Sundy's offer and sat with the large man in the shade drinking the juice. It was bright orange, thick, and tangy.

"Are the dolphins here today?" asked Kelly hopefully.

Sundy cocked his head, looking past Kelly toward the sea.

"There were a couple around earlier," he said, "but I think they've gone now."

"Do the same dolphins help out every day? Can you tell the difference between them? Is there any way to call them?" inquired Kelly.

"Miss Kelly, you've been hanging out with young Jack a little too much. You're starting to sound just like him," laughed Sundy.

Kelly blushed.

"She says a dolphin brought her to the island," said Jack.

"Well, that would be just like them to help a damsel in distress in the sea," remarked Sundy. "Some people say that dolphins are almost as smart as we are and that sometimes they rescue people. Personally, I think they're smarter, though I can think of a few people I might not rescue. But look at the life they lead, playing all day, fishing, and having fun in the sea—who's more intelligent?"

"Sundy, is there any way I can find the dolphin that helped me?" asked Kelly eagerly. If anyone would know, she thought Sundy might.

"Do you remember any special markings on it?" asked the fishkeeper. "I can tell most of them apart by certain scars and the shape of their dorsal fin or tail."

Kelly tried to remember the night following the storm and the dolphin that had towed her to safety.

"I remember its eye looking at me. It looked very kind, but other than that, I can't think of anything. Do the same dolphins hang around here all the time?"

"There's a pod of about twenty that seem to live here. It's rare that you see all of them together. I think they mostly hang out on the other side of the reef. About half of them come regularly to fish."

"If they're mostly outside the reef, they must know a way across," said Kelly.

"Yeah," said Jack quickly, shaking his head, "they know how to swim through the narrow channels on the reef crest and they can jump over where it's really shallow."

"But then how did the dolphin bring me through?" questioned Kelly.

Sundy rubbed his very bald head.

"That's a good point, Kelly," he said. "I'm not sure."

"Why are you so interested in this dolphin anyway?" asked Jack curiously.

"I...I just want to thank it for saving me," answered Kelly.

"Well, you are more than welcome to come by here anytime and see if they're fishing," said Sundy kindly. "You could also go to iguana beach. A few often go there to play or to fish. Or you could go to the scratching spot and see if any dolphin is particularly interested in you. Jack, you know the scratching spot. Oh, and you might bring Paroe with you. For some reason, animals seem to show up when she's around. She has quite the way with them, that little one."

Sundy looked up at the sky and the position of the sun.

"Oh my, it's getting late," he said. "I've got to get some food in the pools. You two take care. Come back anytime for a visit."

Jack and Kelly said goodbye and headed back to the village.

"What's the scratching spot?" asked Kelly.

"To the north of here," said Jack, pointing toward the reef where it curved around the island, "is a spot on the back reef where the dolphins dive down and rub their backs in the sand. We call it the scratching spot because everyone thinks it's how they scratch their backs."

"Can you take me there?" asked Kelly eagerly.

"I suppose we could get a boat and go. But the dolphins aren't always there."

"Can we go tomorrow?"

"Sure, I don't see why not. I doubt Paroe will be able to come, though. She probably won't be up for it yet."

"That's okay, I still want to go."

As they headed back to Jack's house, Kelly quizzed him about everything he knew about dolphins and especially the ones that lived around the island.

Jack was more than happy to talk about dolphins; actually he usually seemed happy to talk about anything.

"We learn a lot about dolphins in school," he explained. "They're mammals in that they breathe air and give birth to live young, which they nurse. But even though they're mammals, dolphins live like fish—you know, doing everything underwater. Did you know that fish move their tails side to side? But dolphins swim by moving their tails up and down. And—"

"What's the sort of *poof* sound I heard them make?" interrupted Kelly.

"Oh, you must have heard them breathing. When dolphins surface, sometimes you hear them inhaling through the blowholes on top of their heads."

"Do they also make a sort of clicking or squeaking sound?"

"Does it sound like this?" asked Jack, and he proceeded to make some weird squeaking noises.

Kelly laughed and shook her head.

"Not exactly." She wasn't sure what he sounded like, but she didn't think it was a dolphin.

"It's how they talk to each another," said Jack. "They also use sound to tell where things are. It's called echolocation. The dolphins send out pulses of sound, that clicking noise you heard, and it hits things, like the reef or fish, and bounces back to them. Inside their heads, they take in the sound and create a picture of whatever's around. Can you imagine if we could do that? Wouldn't need a light at night, that's for sure."

"How does the dolphin turn the sound into a picture?"

"No one really knows," answered Jack, shrugging.

"Do they always eat fish?" asked Kelly, thinking that maybe she could attract them with some food.

"They mostly eat fish, I think, and sometimes maybe squid. They swallow the fish whole, no chewing, and it has to go down the right way, otherwise the fish scales get caught," said Jack, making a gesture as if he were choking.

"When we get in the water with them, they seem to like it if we rub them—except near their blowholes. Don't do that."

"Do you know the ones that live around here?" asked Kelly.

"We can tell a lot of them apart. There's one we call Tee because he has a T-shaped spot of white on his tail. There's also Slash. He's a big male with a long scar running down the back of his head."

"I wish I knew which one helped me."

"Well, maybe you'll remember something if we get in the water with them at the scratching spot tomorrow."

"Has anyone tried to follow the dolphins through the reef?" questioned Kelly.

"People have gone out in boats and tried to watch where they go through, but it's always been places that we can't fit through, especially in a canoe," said Jack. "There really isn't any way off the island, but really, you'll like it here."

Kelly continued to question Jack about the dolphins until they got to his house. Fred the iguana was sitting just outside the doorway. Before going in, Jack scratched the reptile's rough skin and enticed it away from the house with a few flowers.

Dinner was giant clam steaks and tomatoes from the garden. The tomatoes were fresh and tasty, but Kelly discovered that Jack was right; giant clam wasn't very good. It was very chewy on the outside and kind of squishy at the center. She envisioned a peanut butter and jelly sandwich; never before had one seemed like such a delicious treat. She ate the clam to be polite and because she was very hungry.

After a busy day exploring the island and her ordeal earlier in the cave, Kelly was ready for bed soon after dinner. She lay down, thinking. Tomorrow she'd go see Hank again, hopefully to convince him to take her along when he and Pearl left the island. She'd also try to find the dolphin that helped her. She then wondered about Paroe and animals. Everyone seemed to think she had a special connection to them. Maybe once she was feeling better, Paroe could somehow help her find the dolphin. That could be difficult, though, because she couldn't tell her the real reason she wanted to find it. But if Kelly could somehow find the creature that helped her come to the island, maybe the dolphin would know that she wanted to leave and would help her again.

15

The next morning at breakfast, Kelly needed an excuse to go to the treehouse.

"I was thinking of going to see Paroe again this morning, if that's okay."

She wasn't really sure that Paroe was even still there.

"Sure, Jack can go with you if you'd like," said Mrs. Pesca.

"No, no, he's been great," said Kelly. "No reason to wake him, and besides, he doesn't have to babysit me. I'm sure he has better things to do. Later we might go see the dolphins at the scratching spot. Just tell him I'll catch up with him in a little bit. Thanks."

Kelly grabbed some fruit, careful to avoid the papaya, and said good-bye to Mrs. Pesca. This time she knew exactly which way to go and was standing at the base of the treehouse in no time. She walked up the ramp and knocked lightly.

"Hello, anyone home?"

She was expecting an answer from inside the house, but instead a voice came from below.

"Hey there, Kelly," said Hank from the bottom of the treehouse ramp. "How about we walk a little and talk along the way?"

"Sure," said Kelly, walking back down. "How's Paroe?"

"She's doing wonderfully," he answered. "Should be back to her old self by tomorrow."

Hank led them past the house into the forest. He stopped at a large tree with bark that was peeling, red and paper-thin.

"You know what they call this?" he said, chuckling. "The sunburn tree. Of course, its real name is a gumbo-limbo tree."

Kelly wasn't really listening. She was thinking about what she could say to convince him to take her along when he and Pearl left the island.

"What was that?" she asked distractedly. "Oh, I get it, red, peeling… sunburn, that's funny. I…I was thinking that maybe I could find the dolphin that brought me to the island and it could show us a safe way across the reef."

"That would be a big help," said Hank, "but it's pretty unlikely. First you'd have to figure out which dolphin helped you. Then you'd have to get it to show you where you came through."

Kelly knew he was probably right, but she wanted so badly to go home and to see her parents.

"Please take me with you," she pleaded. "It's nice here and all, but I have to go home. I'm a good swimmer and I could help paddle."

"It is just too dangerous," replied Hank, shaking his head. "I'm sorry. Both Pearl and I would never forgive ourselves if something happened to you."

"Oh please. I must go."

"I'm sorry, Kelly, it's just not possible."

"If I can find a way through the reef, will you take me then?"

Hank thought for a moment.

"Well, yes, I suppose if you found a safe way across the reef, you could come. But remember, we're leaving with the spring tide. That's only a week away."

"I know," said Kelly hopefully, "but maybe I can find the way across before then."

"Just don't say anything to anyone about us going. Pearl is having a hard enough time as it is. If Skip and Paroe knew she was planning to leave, it would be even worse."

Kelly assured Hank she wouldn't say a word about their plan.

He walked her back to the treehouse.

"I'm very sorry, Kelly," he said kindly, "but I'm sure you will grow to love it here."

"Is it okay if I come back in a few days? Maybe you'll change your mind."

"You can come back anytime you want, but I don't think we'll change our minds."

Kelly waved goodbye and headed back to the village. Now she just had to find that dolphin and the way through the reef; it was her only chance to go home.

~   ~   ~

All of the canoes on Dolphin Island were built and maintained by the village boatmasters. They were the island's experts in canoe construction and repair. No one owned his or her boat individually. They all shared. That meant if a canoe was available, Jack could take one. However, since he was three years shy of sixteen, Jack needed another person, his age or older, to go along. So that afternoon, on their way to see if a boat was available, Jack and Kelly stopped at Trig and Angel's house, hoping that Trig could join them. She was outside weeding the garden when they arrived.

"Hi Trig, we're going to see if there's a boat to go to the scratching spot," said Jack. "Kelly wants to look for the dolphin that brought her here. Want to come?"

Trig stood up and brushed the sand from her legs and hands.

"Sure, that'd be great," she said. "Any excuse to go in the water."

There was a good breeze blowing onshore, but it was still hot in the midday sun. The three of them were just leaving when Angel came out of the house.

"Hey, where are you guys going?" he questioned. "Trying to sneak away, are we?"

Kelly wished Jack would keep his mouth shut just this once.

"We're gonna see if there's a boat to go out to the scratching spot."

"Why the heck are you going there? Nothing but sand," said Angel smugly.

"Oh, we're just showing Kelly around some more," answered Trig quickly. "Aren't you supposed to be helping Dad rebuild the wall out back?"

"He's just about got it done. He'll never know if I leave. Besides, you'll need my help paddling all the way out there."

"Is it far?" asked Kelly.

"Not with me along," boasted Angel.

With each obnoxious comment, Kelly's dislike of Angel grew.

The four of them went to the beach to find a canoe. There were only three boats left. All the others had been taken out already or were being worked on in the boatyard. One canoe was too small for the four of them. Another was way too big, and it would take a Herculean effort to paddle to the scratching spot. The remaining canoe was the right size, but looked in need of some serious repair. The bench seats were sagging, its paint was faded and chipped, and there were hunks of wood missing in several places.

"We might have to wait till tomorrow," said Jack, looking at the worn-out canoe. "I'm not so sure about this boat."

"C'mon, don't be such a baby," mocked Angel. "It looks fine to me, and besides, they wouldn't have left it on the beach if it wasn't okay to use."

"I guess you're right," agreed Jack a bit hesitantly.

Trig looked a little skeptical. But of the four of them, Kelly was the most worried. The boat looked as though it might leak or, worse, simply fall apart while they were out at the reef. She had done so well up to that point being brave. She didn't want the others to think that she was scared, so she agreed to go.

"Okay, everyone in. Jack, you take the stern. I'll take the bow. Trig and Kelly, you get in the middle," barked Angel.

They pushed the canoe into the water and everyone climbed in. There were four paddles in the boat.

"Well, at least it's not sinking," noted Jack jokingly.

Kelly sensed that Jack was a little nervous too and somehow it made her feel better not to be the only one.

"C'mon now, it's fine. Don't get wimpy on me, just paddle," said Angel.

Trig showed Kelly how to paddle with short smooth strokes. After a while she got the hang of it and fell into a rhythm with the others.

It was a partly cloudy, hot day with a moderate breeze blowing onshore. The old boat moved sluggishly through the water and against the wind. They were making progress, but it was hard work.

"Stroke...stroke...c'mon, you ladies, pull," ordered Angel.

Trig looked at Kelly and rolled her eyes, silently apologizing for her twin.

The breeze made it a little choppy in the lagoon, and every so often the canoe would hit a wave just right and water splashed into their faces. Kelly wasn't sure that this was one adventure worth having. Between the waves, the worn-out canoe, and Angel bossing them around, she thought that maybe the trip was a mistake.

"Maybe we should just go to iguana beach instead," she whispered to Jack.

"It's just a little choppy. I think we'll be fine," he replied, though with little enthusiasm.

"Don't be such worrywarts," shouted Angel. "This is nothing. But to make it easier on you lightweights, let's head for the smooth water behind the reef. It'll be easier for you to paddle there."

For once, Kelly thought he'd said something that made sense. The reef crest broke the incoming waves and the wind chop in the lagoon didn't start for another thirty feet, so there was a channel of calm water that ran along the back of the reef. It took another twenty minutes of hard paddling, but then they were in the smooth water tucked in behind the reef. The group rested for a few minutes and then headed north, following the inside of the reef as it curved around the island.

"Hey look, there's Sundy at the sea pools," said Jack, pointing toward shore.

They waved, but Sundy was busy and didn't see the four kids in the old canoe heading north.

Kelly's arms were getting tired, but she didn't want to quit while everyone else paddled. She gritted her teeth and kept at it. Finally Angel pointed ahead.

"There we are," he said. "A few more strokes and we'll be at the spot. Right Trig? Isn't that the place, just ahead?"

"Yup, that's it," said Jack, before Trig could answer.

They stopped paddling and glided up to an area on the back reef where the coral formed a horseshoe-shaped notch. It was about ten feet deep. Angel jumped off the boat with the bow line in hand and dove down. After tying it off on the reef, he came back and grabbed onto the side of the boat.

"One of my expert knots as always," he boasted.

"Oh brother," said Trig, shaking her head.

Kelly looked around expectantly, hoping to see some dolphins, but there were none in sight.

"They might come while we're swimming," said Jack.

Without any hesitation this time, Kelly jumped in. While the other three teenagers dove and swam around, she stayed mostly at the surface, floating and looking for dolphins. She even tried to listen for their telltale squeaks and clicks. Every once in a while she'd dive under a few feet and look around, thinking maybe she'd see them underwater. Everything was still blurry, but she peered searchingly into the blue around her. Nothing. She continued to look and listen, hoping the dolphins would come to scratch their backs.

While they were swimming about, hoping the dolphins would arrive, a strong squall was developing just offshore. It wasn't a huge storm, but it was intense, built from the day's heat. And the onshore wind was blowing the thunderstorm toward the island and the group of teenagers swimming on the back reef.

A shadow crept across the seafloor as thick clouds rolled in. The sea darkened and the reef's colors, usually so brilliant in the sun, became muted and dull. And as the wind began to strengthen, the waves breaking on the reef crest got bigger and louder.

Trig swam to a shallow sandy spot and stood up, looking around. Just offshore, dark-gray mushroom-shaped clouds were bulging skyward. Below the clouds, rain streaked downward. A bolt of lightning pierced the sky.

"Hey guys, a bad squall's moving in," yelled Trig. "Come on, let's get going. Back to the boat."

Jack and Angel were a ways down the reef and didn't hear her. Kelly was nearby. She had been so intent on looking and listening for dolphins that she hadn't seen the storm brewing in the distance. Now that she did, she headed quickly for the canoe.

Trig helped her into the boat.

"It's okay; these squalls come through all the time," she said reassuringly. "And with this wind, we'll put the sail up and be back at the beach in no time."

They heard the deep rolling rumble of distant thunder.

"Angel, Jack," yelled Trig. "C'mon guys, we gotta go in."

This time Jack heard the girl's yells and nudged Angel. The two of them started swimming for the canoe. Just then, the wind grew noticeably stronger and the canoe strained on the line tied to the reef. Suddenly, the line whipped free and the strong wind took the canoe, pushing it rapidly away from the reef.

Trig picked up one of the paddles.

"Kelly, grab a paddle," she shouted. "Jack and Angel will never catch us if the wind takes us too fast."

The two girls struggled to paddle against the strong wind in the old canoe. They were drifting further away, fast. Jack and Angel were now swimming as hard as they could to catch up. But the squall was moving in and the wind got even stronger. They saw a flash of lightning, and a loud boom of thunder confirmed that the storm was getting closer. Steep, choppy waves now filled the lagoon.

"Keep paddling," yelled Trig over the howling wind.

Kelly was stroking as hard as she could, but they weren't making any progress. Instead, they were being blown away from the reef and the two boys. It reminded Kelly of her ordeal in the storm at sea, but she had no time to be scared. She had to keep paddling, though it seemed no use. She and Trig in the old canoe were just no match for the wind. Jack and Angel were getting farther away.

Then, quite unexpectedly, they started making progress. The boat was moving back toward the reef and the two teenage boys. For each stroke the two girls took, the canoe moved smoothly forward. Even when their paddles were in the air mid-stroke, the boat strangely glided forward, cutting through the lagoon's steep chop. Trig and Kelly held up their paddles and the boat continued to move against the wind. The two girls stared at one another in amazement.

"Look over the bow," yelled Trig. "It's the dolphins!"

There, in front of the canoe, were three dolphins. The one in the middle had the bow line in its beak and was pulling the canoe toward the boys. Within just a few minutes Angel and Jack were within reach of the boat. The dolphin released the line.

Trig and Kelly helped the boys into the canoe. But there was no time to thank the dolphins or even catch their breath. Immediately, the strong wind grabbed the boat again and started pushing it toward shore. The squall was even closer now. A bolt of lightning tore through the sky and the sharp crack of thunder rang out. And the rain was swiftly coming their way; it already hid the reef in a heavy curtain of water.

Trig stood up and looked toward the island.

"If we don't get further south," she urged, "the wind will crash us onto the rocks. We've got to head south to the beach. Start paddling and fast."

Angel picked up his paddle and sneered at Trig.

"Thanks a lot for leaving us, sis," he said. "Now look at the mess we're in."

"We didn't leave you on purpose," she snapped back. "*Someone* didn't tie the boat off very well and it got loose."

"Look, there's Sundy," shouted Jack, pointing toward shore. "Maybe he'll see us."

"A whole lot of good that will do us out here," muttered Angel.

Kelly kept paddling, her arms aching. They were making a little progress, but not enough. She looked toward shore and got a closer look at what Trig was so worried about. The wind was blowing them toward a section of the coast lined with jagged black rock.

"Ahh, guys we have another problem," said Jack, pointing to the water now rising in the canoe. To make matters worse, small leaks had developed in the old boat and seawater was beginning to pool at its floor.

"Oh man," said Angel, "I knew this canoe wasn't any good."

Jack, Trig, and Kelly looked unbelievingly at Angel.

Oh, shut up already," yelled Trig. "Just keep paddling."

They were now a hundred feet from shore. The wind was driving them toward the rocks and steep waves rolled the canoe crazily from side to side. The water inside was getting deeper and it was getting even harder to paddle and to steer. Kelly looked up and saw Sundy down the beach. He was frantically waving them away from the rocks. She thought she might have heard a high-pitched whistle come from the beach, but it was hard to tell in the screaming wind.

At first they felt just a few drops, and then the rain came down in torrents. Within minutes they were drenched. None of them could see farther than ten feet in front of the boat, which was filling up even faster with water. Another flash of lightning and a piercing crack of thunder, and the rocks looked hideously close. Kelly was shaking, her eyes wide with fear; she was sure that in just minutes they would be smashed to pieces on the rocks.

Then, just as before, the boat started gliding smoothly. Instead of being pushed with the wind, they were being pulled sideways against it. They all stopped paddling, looked at one another, and all together leaned toward the bow, gazing over the side. There again were the three dolphins, with one towing them by the line from the boat's bow. With each up-and-down sweep of its tail, the dolphin easily pulled the now waterlogged canoe and its occupants through the waves.

Jack dropped his paddle and let out a long sigh of relief.

"Oh, thank goodness," said Trig.

Kelly could only nod in agreement.

"Oh come on, we weren't in any *real* danger," said Angel.

"Yeah right, I don't want to think about what would have happened if we had hit those rocks in this wind. No thanks to you," snapped Trig, wiping the rain from her face.

Kelly leaned over the side of the canoe trying to get a closer look at the dolphins. She put her hand over her eyes to block the rain. Were there any distinguishing marks on the animals? She thought she saw a scar running down the head of one of the dolphins, and the one towing the boat had a little notch in its dorsal fin. Had she seen that before? Could it be the same dolphin from the night of the storm?

Soon the rain began to let up and the thunder turned to a distant rumble. Visibility improved. They were just twenty feet from shore. The dolphin let go of the line.

"Look, we've passed the rocks," observed Jack as he paddled toward the beach. Sundy waded out and helped pull the boat onto the sand.

"A nasty squall. You should have come straight in. What happened out there?" asked the plump fishkeeper, his caterpillar eyebrows scrunched low on his forehead.

"Nothing serious, we just got caught off guard, that's all," said Angel.

The three others in the boat looked at Angel and shook their heads, but said nothing.

Kelly was a little shaken, but that didn't matter because she had gotten a good look at the dolphins.

"Hey Sundy," she said. "The dolphins, they helped again."

"Sometimes they come when needed most," noted Sundy smiling.

"Did you call them?" asked Jack suspiciously.

"Maybe they just knew you needed help. Besides, seems Miss Kelly here has a history of being rescued by a dolphin. I'd say she fits in well on Dolphin Island."

"Do you think one of them was the same one that helped me the other night?" asked Kelly.

"Hard to say," responded Sundy. "Did you recognize anything about them?"

The sky was getting even brighter and the rain had turned to just a slight drizzle. Kelly looked out into the lagoon. There was no sign of the dolphins. They had disappeared as quickly as they had come.

"One of them had a sort of notch in its fin," said Kelly.

"That's Nicki, she's here a lot. She's a young female, likes to play. Maybe she was the one that helped you get to the island."

Soon the sun broke through the clouds and the wind died down completely. Once again the lagoon was calm. Now they needed to get the canoe back to the beach in front of the village. Sundy helped them bail the water out of the boat, and he found some old netting to temporarily plug up a few of the holes.

"Don't think that will stop all the leaks," he said, "but if you paddle or walk it back in shallow water, you should be okay."

The four of them said good-bye to Sundy. Having done plenty of paddling for one day, they decided to walk the canoe back along the beach. It wasn't easy, but it was better than more paddling. By the time they got back, all four were thoroughly exhausted as well as soaking wet from the storm.

"That's enough adventure for me for one day," noted Jack, talking at a surprisingly normal speed.

"Me too," added Kelly and Trig in unison.

Angel was quiet. Working together, they pushed and pulled the canoe up onto the beach where they had found it.

"I'm going to tell the boatmasters this canoe needs fixing," barked Angel grumpily.

"C'mon, Angel, let's go home," said Trig, shaking her head. "See you guys around."

"See ya," said Kelly.

Trig and Angel left for their house. Kelly and Jack headed home as well.

"I'm really sorry about that," apologized Jack. "We don't usually get caught in a squall like that. I mean, squalls happen a lot, but usually we can get in pretty quick. I mean, I'm not really sure how that happened. Angel did sort of screw up with the tie line and the boat was sort of leaky and—"

"It's okay, Jack," interrupted Kelly, noting that his talking speed had already returned to normal. "Hey, I got to see the dolphins again. Maybe Nicki was the one that helped me get to the island. Do you think we could go to iguana beach tomorrow and see if she'll show up there?"

"Sure, maybe Paroe will even be up for it. The dolphins seem to come more often when she's around."

"What's the scoop with her and animals anyway?"

"I don't know," answered Jack, shrugging. "It's almost like they're attracted to her and I swear sometimes it's like she knows what they're thinking."

"Do you think she can talk to them?"

"Don't know."

For the rest of the walk home, Jack and Kelly were quiet. Jack was tired and felt bad about getting Kelly caught in the storm. Kelly, on the other hand, wasn't even thinking about the storm. She was wishing she could talk to animals and in particular to Nicki, the dolphin with the notch in its fin. She'd ask the dolphin if it had saved her and, if so, how it had come through the reef. If Paroe came with them to iguana beach tomorrow and Nicki showed up, maybe she really could find a way through the reef.

16

The following day, after Kelly helped Jack with his morning chores, they got Paroe, who was feeling much better, and set off for iguana beach. Kelly was excited about seeing the dolphins again, though she wasn't so sure about a beach full of iguanas. They walked south through the village until they came to a wide swampy area with a series of wooden walkways built over it.

After a good night's rest, Jack was back in full force.

"So, this is our wetland," he explained. "You know…where the village waste streams come. Over there you can see where they flow in. The plants and soil filter out the nasty stuff in the water. The wetland is pretty big. It runs into the mangroves." He was pointing to a forest of short, odd-looking trees.

As they walked along the wooden boardwalk, Jack identified different plants. Several times, Paroe quietly corrected him when he made a mistake, but he hardly even noticed.

"How do you know so many of the plants?" asked Kelly. "At home, I can barely tell the difference between an oak and a maple tree."

"We have a class in plants at school," answered Jack.

"My Mom taught me," added Paroe, "because she uses plants for medicine. See, this one over here, it's a white mangrove and we use the bark to treat skin rashes."

"It's this way," said Jack, taking a left at an intersection on the boardwalk. "Paroe showed you the white mangrove. There are also black and red mangroves, though they aren't really red, black, or white. Well, the reds are kind of red. Anyway, the white mangroves like it pretty dry—see how round their leaves are. Over here where it's muddy, that's the black mangrove. Its leaves are a little pointier. And see all those black tips sticking up through the mud? They're part of the tree—sort of like breathing tubes."

Kelly looked down in the mud and sure enough, at the base of the trees, there were hundreds of small twigs poking up through the mud.

Paroe tore off a small cluster of white flowers from the black mangrove tree and handed them to Kelly.

"Taste 'em," she said.

Kelly looked at the flowers in her hand. She had never eaten flowers before. She looked skeptically at the blooms, shrugged, and then popped them into her mouth.

"They taste like…like honey."

Jack plucked a leaf off the black mangrove and passed it to Kelly.

"I hope you don't want me to eat this too," said Kelly.

"No, just feel the bottom of the leaf," he said. "Feels sort of crusty, doesn't it?"

"Yeah, like there's sand on it or something."

"Nope, not sand, it's salt," announced Jack. "The water here is a little salty, and when the plants take it in, they need to get rid of the salt—so it comes out on the leaves."

"I didn't know plants could do that," said Kelly, wondering if they had plants like that at home, her home.

"Even better is the red mangrove. See the one over there in the water with the weird roots hanging down?" said Jack, pointing to a tree whose trunk became a tangle of thick, orange, branch-like roots hanging down into the water.

Kelly walked over to one of the odd-looking trees next to the boardwalk. She felt its leaves.

"It's in the same water, but the leaf doesn't feel salty?"

"Nope," said Jack, smirking slightly. "They do it differently. There are special valves on their roots that take in water, but leave the salt behind."

"What about those skinny green things hanging down from the tree?" asked Kelly. "They look kinda like Christmas tree ornaments."

"They're the baby mangroves, seedlings really," answered Paroe. "They fall off the tree and float around for a while, and when they hit land, they put roots down and start growing."

"You guys sure know a lot about mangroves," remarked Kelly, thinking that if she did have to stay on the island, there would be a lot to learn. But she didn't want to think that way. She just had to find a way to go home.

Jack pointed into the water between the roots of the red mangrove.

"See all the small fish swimming around the roots?" he said. "It's like a nursery for the babies. When the fish get older, they swim out and live on the reef."

They continued down the boardwalk through the mangroves. It was shady, but the trees blocked the breeze coming off the ocean.

"Man, it's hot in here, and what's that stench?" said Kelly, holding her nose. "Smells kinda like rotten eggs."

"It's the mud and plant stuff rotting," said Jack. "Supposed to be a good thing, but I think it just stinks. C'mon, the beach is just ahead."

In minutes they came to a short, narrow beach. They hopped off the boardwalk and walked along the sand. Kelly was amazed by the tremendous number of seashells lying in piles on the beach. She bent down and picked up a beautiful tan-and-white spiraled shell with thin brown stripes running around it.

"Look at all these shells," she said in wonderment. "People at home would go crazy collecting here."

"You should see this place after a really big storm," said Paroe. "There are even more shells, and sometimes coral and sponge wash up too."

Just then, about five large iguanas came running out of the shrubs at the back of the beach. Startled, Kelly ran down to the water's edge away from the scurrying creatures. Paroe and Jack stayed where they were. The iguanas stopped about five feet from them and tilted their heads from side to side, looking curiously at the two-legged creatures on the beach.

Two of the iguanas approached Paroe more closely. She knelt down and they came even nearer. She scratched their heads.

"C'mon, don't worry about them," said Jack, heading down the beach.

Kelly followed, warily eyeing the iguanas that were now trailing behind Paroe like a small pack of dogs. They walked down the beach until they came to what looked almost like the beginning of a paved roadway. Broad flat rocks, like large floor tiles, sat in a row leading up to a rocky cliff.

"Is this an old road?" asked Kelly curiously.

"Nah," replied Jack, "it's just beachrock. The sand gets hardened into rock as seawater splashes it, drains down, and then dries up—the minerals left behind act kind of like cement. We learned that in school too."

Kelly looked down as they walked over the beachrock. She saw shells and pieces of coral cemented into the square blocks. Up ahead, sprawled out on the flat rocks at the base of the cliff, were at least twenty small black iguanas. Some of them were lying on top of one another, forming bizarre little piles of the strange-looking reptiles.

Kelly stopped and stared at the creatures.

"Those are the marine iguanas," said Jack, hanging back a bit. "See the difference? They're smaller and darker than the land ones. They go into the ocean to eat and then come out and soak up the sun to get warm. But don't get too close, unless you like *lizard snot*."

"Yeah," added Paroe. "They eat algae and take in too much salt… kinda like the mangroves, only they sneeze it out their noses."

As if on cue, Kelly heard a sound somewhat akin to several people spitting and then she felt something wet hit her leg.

"*Yuck!*" exclaimed Kelly as she jumped back, getting out of reach of the flying lizard snot.

"Happens all the time if you get too close," laughed Jack. "Ready for a swim?"

Kelly grimaced, nodded, and wiped the goo from her leg. She then gazed out over the lagoon, looking for the rise of a fin or the telltale spouting from a dolphin's blowhole. Nothing. She looked over at Paroe, who was also peering out over the water.

"Do you think they'll come, Paroe?" asked Kelly.

"Hard to say. Some days they show up, other days they don't."

"Can you really tell what they're thinking or talk to them?" questioned Kelly hopefully.

"I'm not really sure. Sometimes it does seem like I know what they're thinking or trying to say."

They waded into the water. The ocean was clear and cool. Kelly went about shoulder-deep and floated for a few minutes. She stood up, looking and listening for the dolphins. Still nothing. Jack and Paroe seemed less concerned with being on the lookout for dolphins. They dove in and swam over a bed of seagrass, pointing out a large stingray resting in the undersea meadow. Then, they searched under the ledges of nearby rocks and yelled to Kelly when they spotted an interesting fish or, in one case, a large green moray eel.

Soon a small school of fish trailed Paroe as she swam. A few even nibbled gently at her legs. She seemed completely unaware of it or the fact that the fish didn't do the same thing with either Jack or Kelly.

Kelly watched in awe as a large parrotfish swam up to Paroe and allowed the girl to reach out and stroke its beautiful turquoise body. Paroe pulled some algae off the bottom and fed it to the fish. The parrotfish had large white buckteeth, just as Jack had described. She then scanned the lagoon again for any sign of the dolphins. Still nothing.

After about an hour Kelly began to shiver. Her fingers were getting white and wrinkly. She waded back up the beach and sat on the beachrock, warming up in the bright sun. She looked around to make sure she wasn't in sneezing range of any of the marine iguanas. Jack and Paroe were still swimming; they appeared to be chasing something.

Paroe looked up, saw Kelly, and headed for the beach. She sat down next to her.

"Don't worry," she said. "You'll see them again. We can come back tomorrow if you want."

"Okay," replied Kelly, trying not to be disappointed. She wished she could tell Paroe why she wanted so badly to find the dolphin, why she wanted to find a way across the reef.

"I wish I could find out how the dolphin brought me here," remarked Kelly, trying to sound as if it didn't matter to her as much as it did.

"Why do you want to know that?" asked Paroe.

Kelly was now skating on thin ice; she had to be very careful not to say too much, but Paroe might be able to help her.

"Well, if…ahh…we ever wanted to go across the reef."

"It's way too dangerous, and besides, why would anyone want to leave Dolphin Island?" said Paroe, but as soon as she said it, she looked down and added, "I'm sorry, you probably want to go home and see your parents. But really, you'll like it here with us, and I think Jack likes having you around. It's like he has a sister now."

Just then, Jack yelled from the water, "Hey, check this baby out."

He was holding up a big spiny lobster. It was an enormous one, and Jack needed both hands just to hold on to it. Then without warning, the lobster began madly flapping its tail. Jack struggled to hold on, but the lobster was too big and too strong. It jumped out of his hands and Jack tumbled backward into the water.

Paroe and Kelly both laughed.

"Our great hunter, Jack," said Paroe.

Jack was now swiveling around, trying to figure out where the lobster had gone.

"C'mon, forget about it," shouted Paroe. "We can't take it anyway. Let's go...looks like the dolphins have better things to do today."

"We can't take lobsters on our own," she added, talking to Kelly. "The village council controls how much is collected and who can hunt. That way, we don't take too many."

Jack walked out of the water toward them, shaking his head and holding his hand. "*Shoot!*" he cursed. "One of those blasted urchins got me."

When he held out his finger, Kelly saw a swelling red welt with a small black dot at its center.

"Well, you know what to do," said Paroe, chuckling.

"Yeah, yeah...turn around," grumbled Jack.

Paroe snickered and grabbed Kelly's arm, and together they turned their backs to Jack.

"He's not really going to pee on it, is he?" asked Kelly.

"Oh yes he is," Paroe said. "It helps dissolve the tip of the spine that's stuck in his finger."

"That's really gross," said Kelly, and the two girls fell into a fit of giggles.

"Are you two done laughing?" said Jack seriously. "You know, it's not funny. This hurts."

They turned around and saw Jack standing there, having just peed on his finger, with his hands on his hips looking very serious, and they started giggling all over again.

After Jack dried off a bit and the two girls finally stopped laughing, the three of them walked back to the village, making plans to return the following day.

17

Kelly, Jack, and Paroe returned to iguana beach each of the following two days, hoping the dolphins would come, but still none appeared. Kelly was beginning to panic. She only had a few days left before Hank and Pearl would leave the island, without her.

On the third day it was cloudy and threatening to rain, but Kelly had convinced Paroe and Jack to try again. The three of them stood on the beachrock looking out toward the reef in the distance and the white foam where waves were breaking at its crest. Nearby, a pile of marine iguanas lay, occasionally releasing a spray of salty liquid.

"School starts in a few days," Jack told Kelly. "You'll like it."

"I suppose," she answered, surveying the lagoon for signs of the dolphins. "So why do you think they haven't shown up?"

"They've probably just been busy elsewhere, but they'll come," said Paroe confidently. "Let's go in."

It wasn't a great day for swimming. The cloudy weather made the undersea world look less colorful than usual. But it was still fun for

Kelly, who was now quite comfortable swimming in the ocean and with the blurry look of things underwater. Over the past two days, she had learned a lot from Jack and Paroe. They showed her how to better bend at the waist and dive down underwater. They helped her learn how to hold her breath longer and how to tickle a lobster so that it came out of its hole.

Together the three of them had explored the nooks and crannies of the lagoon, chased sea creatures, and avoided others, and they were fast becoming good friends. Kelly really was beginning to think of Jack almost like a brother and Paroe like one of her close friends at home. As she felt closer to them, she also felt worse and worse about her desire to leave the island and return home, and about keeping Hank's plan a secret from them. But her love for her parents was stronger than any new friendship could ever be.

Kelly, Jack, and Paroe dove into the shallow water and swam over a field of thick-bladed seagrass. Small fish and crabs darted away from the three teenagers. Jack pointed out a sponge that looked like a small orange castle, and Kelly found several scallops resting peacefully on the bottom. From the grass, they cruised over a large patch of sand. A sea turtle was resting on the bottom. They all dove down together and stroked its shell. The turtle seemed startled by their touch, as if woken from a deep sleep. It eyed them briefly, then flapped its hind and fore flippers, taking off in underwater flight.

Kelly swam up to the surface and followed, trying to keep up with the cruising sea creature. Even with its heavy shell, the sea turtle could easily out-swim her, and she lost sight of it within minutes. Just then, Kelly thought she heard a clicking sound.

"Kelly, Kelly, they're here!" shouted Paroe.

Kelly looked up, and just a few feet away there were two dolphins circling Paroe. She and Jack swam over and the dolphins moved away. But it was only for a moment and soon they were back. With a flick of their tails, the animals turned on their sides and glided by. Kelly could swear they were looking right at her. One of the dolphins came up to

Paroe and nuzzled her with its beak; then it swam slowly by, sliding its body lightly against her hand.

Kelly stood transfixed as the other dolphin moved nearer. She extended her hand and touched its sleek, rubbery skin.

"Kelly, check this out," said Jack, extending his hand at the surface.

One of the dolphins swam over and put its dorsal fin perfectly in his hand. With a gentle grasp, Jack tightened his fingers on the dolphin's fin, and in an instant he was lifted off his feet, gliding swiftly through the water.

"C'mon, Kelly, try it. They like to take us for rides," said Paroe, coming over to Kelly and showing her how to put her hand out. Within minutes the other dolphin came by and, just as one had done with Jack, it put its fin in her hand.

"Now hold on, but not too tight," guided Paroe.

Kelly tightened her grip ever so slightly, and before she knew it, she too was whisked away by the dolphin. It was fantastic. She laughed as together they sped through the water, spray splashing into her face. The dolphin slowed, turned, and brought her back to where Paroe and now Jack were standing.

It was Paroe's turn next, and a dolphin came by to sweep her off for a ride.

Kelly was smiling so wide her cheeks hurt.

"That was awesome," she said excitedly. "Do you recognize them?"

Jack squinted, trying to get a better look at the animals.

"I'm not sure about the one with Paroe, but the other one has a notch in its dorsal fin." He pointed at the fin of the dolphin floating nearby.

"Hey, you're right. That's Nicki. The same one that helped us the other day."

The other dolphin dropped Paroe off, and Kelly examined it carefully as it passed by. There was a scar on the dolphin's head; it ran just behind the animal's eye and the back of its mouth.

"That one is definitely Slash," said Jack, pointing to the dolphin as it went by. "See the scar? They all look like they're smiling, but that scar really makes him look like he's grinning."

Kelly looked more closely. Jack was right. The scar at the edge of the dolphin's mouth gave it the appearance of having a wide smile—like how a child would draw the mouth in a happy face. She remembered the night of the storm and recalled how the dolphin had appeared to be smiling—could Slash, not Nicki, be the dolphin that had saved her?

The scarred dolphin swam past Paroe and approached Kelly. It paused just in front of her and then slowly moved closer.

"Rub its beak, they like that," suggested Paroe.

Kelly reached out and touched the dolphin's beak. It came in closer and nuzzled her. She rubbed its gray skin, being careful not to go near the blowhole.

"They don't usually do that on a first meeting," noted Paroe.

Kelly just smiled. It was wonderful being so close to the animal. The dolphin was big and powerful, yet so gentle. Water spouted from the animal's blowhole and it inhaled. The dolphin raised its head, squeaked several times, and then, with a flick of its tail, swam off. The two animals dove down together and disappeared.

"Hey, where'd they go?" asked Kelly, looking all around.

"Watch…they'll come up in a minute to breathe," said Jack.

The three of them scanned the water in the lagoon. A few minutes later the two dolphins came up, their fins breaking the surface. The animals took a breath, water spouting from their blowholes. Then, in unison, they dove down again and headed seaward toward the reef.

"Can we call them back?" asked Kelly.

"I think they have other things to do, probably going fishing," said Paroe.

"Does anyone really know how to talk to them?"

"If anyone can, it's Sundy," said Jack. "He can whistle a lot like they sound. So do you think one of them is the dolphin that saved you?"

"I think it may have been Slash," answered Kelly. "I remember thinking that the dolphin looked like it was smiling."

"Well, it did seem to like you," said Jack, "but you know, they all kind of look like they're smiling."

"No, I think it was Slash," said Paroe. "Didn't you see how it came up to her? They don't usually do that at first."

Once the dolphins were out of sight, the three of them got out of the water and dried off. They sat on the beachrock for a while talking about their swim with the dolphins. Kelly told them it was one of the most incredible things she'd ever done.

On their way back to the village, Kelly thought about the dolphin Slash. If it was the one that had saved her, how could she get it to show her the way through the reef? She wished she could ask Paroe and Jack to help and tell them about Hank's plan. She hated keeping secrets, especially from them. They had been so nice and had become her friends. At least now she could tell Hank that she knew which dolphin had saved her. At least she thought she knew. Time was running out.

18

The next morning Kelly was in the bathroom brushing her teeth when she noticed something different about her hair. The strands falling into her face seemed lighter in color. Her body seemed different too, but she wasn't sure why. Maybe it was just the tan she'd gotten from spending so much time in the sun—even with the stinky sunscreen. She felt braver now, more adventurous like the rest of her family. Did she look different too?

It was just three days until the spring tide and Hank's attempt to leave the island. Kelly wanted to tell him about the dolphin, Slash; maybe it would help convince him to take her along.

As usual, Jack was still asleep when she went into the kitchen for breakfast.

"Good morning, Kelly," said Mrs. Pesca. "What do you and Jack have planned for today? Only a few days left till school starts. You'll like school. You'll learn all sorts of interesting things about the ocean and the island."

"Sounds good," said Kelly, trying to keep the conversation to a minimum.

Several times now, Mrs. Pesca had tried to get Kelly to discuss her parents and her feelings about staying on the island. Kelly had repeatedly found ways to change the subject or suggest that she just wasn't ready to talk about it.

"I think I'll go visit the goats before Jack wakes up. Do you have anything I can feed them?" asked Kelly.

"Sure, take a few carrots. Be careful. I'll tell Jack when he gets up that you'll be back shortly."

She hated lying to Mrs. Pesca too. She also had been so nice.

Kelly ate a few scrambled tortoise eggs, drank some goat's milk, and then took off through the village. She ran nearly the entire way.

She knocked lightly at the treehouse doorway.

"Hello? Hank, are you here?"

"Morning, Kelly," said Hank, coming to the door. "C'mon in."

A large basket sat on the floor, surrounded by an assortment of small woven pouches and shell containers.

"Pearl is off collecting plants. She wants to leave a good stock for Paroe and the others in the village when she goes. I'm getting some of our food and supplies together for the trip."

"How about some carrots to take?" asked Kelly, adding hopefully, "Have you thought anymore about me going with you?"

"Sorry Kelly," replied Hank. "We haven't changed our minds. It is just too dangerous."

"But I think I've found the dolphin that brought me to the island. It's the one called Slash."

"That's wonderful, really, but it doesn't change things. You still need to get this dolphin to show you how to go across the reef."

"I...I know," stuttered Kelly. "But maybe if you take me, Slash will help, just like he did before. Oh, please take me. I have to see my parents again."

She didn't want to cry and hadn't for days, but tears were beginning to fill her eyes and she had a large lump in her throat. Hank looked at the young girl with tears now sliding down her cheeks.

"Oh please, please don't cry," implored Hank. "I've always been such a sucker for tears."

Kelly couldn't help it; her bottom lip was now quivering and her eyes continued to well up.

"Okay, okay," sighed Hank. "I'll tell you what. I'm going to try the boat out tomorrow night as sort of a dress rehearsal. I plan to take it out and paddle around the lagoon on the opposite side of the island. It'll be late at night. But if you want, you can come. Pearl wants to spend her last night here with her kids and I could use another hand. Who knows, maybe your dolphin friend will come and show us this hidden passage through the reef."

"Oh yes, I'll come, definitely," said Kelly, wiping her face.

Hank proceeded to explain to Kelly where and when to meet him the following night. He reminded her again not to tell anyone and that if she didn't make it he would understand.

Kelly walked back to the Pescas' house determined to sneak out the next night and meet Hank. She would go with him while he tested the boat. Even if Slash didn't show up, she could show him that she could paddle and help out. This was her chance, but she'd have to figure out how to get out of the Pescas' house without anyone, especially Jack, noticing. She felt bad about sneaking out on Jack, but it just couldn't be helped, not if she really wanted to go home.

~   ~   ~

Kelly spent the rest of the day with Jack and Paroe. They worked in the gardens, swam at the beach, and even chased a few land crabs. Kelly was both excited and nervous about going out in Hank's boat the next night and wished she could tell her new friends about it.

--------------- **19** ---------------

The next morning Kelly lay in bed thinking about how to sneak out that night. She'd need some sort of flashlight to find her way to meet Hank, and she'd have to get out of the house without anyone waking up. The second part might not be so hard; Jack seemed to sleep soundly, and Mr. and Mrs. Pesca typically closed their door at night. She'd just have to chance it and be very quiet. But she did need a light. She could take one of the light orbs from the house, but they were pretty big and awfully bright. Then an idea came to her. It would be dangerous. She'd have to get away from Jack during the day to get what she needed. But it might just work. She'd just have to risk it.

~   ~   ~

As luck would have it, that day Jack was going out to the reef with his father to spearfish. They asked Kelly if she wanted to come—in fact,

Jack had been rather persistent—but Kelly had convincingly explained that she wasn't quite ready for spearfishing.

After Jack and Mr. Pesca left, Mrs. Pesca put her arm around Kelly.

"I'm so glad you're here," she said. "It's so nice to have you living with us."

"Thanks. Ahh...I was thinking I'd go see Paroe," said Kelly. "Can I take them some fruit? Their garden still isn't doing very well."

"By all means, take some carrots and tomatoes as well. We've got plenty."

Kelly went into her room and grabbed a basket in which to carry the fruit. She also took an extra wrap from the foot of her bed.

"Go ahead and take some fruit and vegetables from the kitchen," said Mrs. Pesca on her way into the bathroom.

Along with a few mangoes, bananas, carrots, and some tomatoes, Kelly took a coiled shell glass from a shelf over the sink and a coconut shell container from below, hoping no one would notice that either was missing. She put all of it in her basket and headed to the Aguans' house.

Skip and Paroe were both outside working on the garden, or what was supposed to be a garden. It was still mostly weeds and dirt.

"Hi," said Kelly.

"Hey Kelly," answered Paroe. Skip looked up and nodded.

"Mrs. Pesca sent over some extra mangoes and stuff. They've got lots."

"We don't need handouts," grumbled Skip, frowning. "It's just taking a little while to get the garden going again, that's all."

"Don't listen to him," said Paroe. "That'll be great, thank Jack's mom for us. Want some water or something?"

"No thanks. Just came by to drop this off," said Kelly. "I've got some stuff to do before school starts. Mrs. Pesca gave me some books to read, since I'll be sort of behind."

She hated lying to Paroe, but she couldn't tell her where she was really going or why. She handed her the fruits and vegetables and said good-bye.

Kelly left, feeling guilty and nervous. She headed through the village to the trail that went to the animal farms and waterfall pool. Within minutes she was at the place where the path split. This time she took the wrong trail on purpose, the one to the left. As before, the path soon became overgrown and the light began to dim. Then in the distance she saw the blue glow. The soft blue light cast a shadow at the cave's entrance. She thought back to her last venture into the cave and rubbed her bottom. Who knew what would have happened if she'd fallen into the glowing pool or been caught in the cave. She'd have to be more careful this time.

Standing outside the cave's entrance, her legs felt like rubber and her hands were sticky with sweat. If she wanted to go home, she'd have to do this. She took a couple of deep breaths, looked around to be sure that no one was watching, and climbed through the opening.

She heard faint voices in the distance. This time Kelly moved painstakingly slowly, staying as quiet as possible. The rocks were as slippery as before and her heart was beating fast. She slowly worked her way down, around the pillars and piles of smooth tan stone in the cave. Several times she nearly slipped, but this time she was prepared and had a good handhold. As before, an eerie blue glow emanated from the water at the bottom of the cave. Kelly wasn't sure if it was even safe to touch.

Finally, when she'd made it to the water's edge, Kelly looked for a place with safe footing. Then, from the basket she had slung across her shoulder, she took out the coiled shell glass and coconut shell container. She carefully dipped each into the pool, filling them with the glowing water. She placed the lid on the coconut shell and put the extra wrap she had brought around the coiled shell so that it was covered and would stand upright in the basket.

Then, very, very carefully, Kelly climbed back up, carrying the basket and its contents out of the cave. She went even slower on the way up than on the journey down. One slip and the people at the other end of the cave might hear her or she could end up in the pool at the cave's bottom. The climb was nerve-wracking, and as Kelly got tired, it seemed harder to find sure footing. Twice she slipped and heard the water slosh in the containers in the basket. She hoped it hadn't all spilled out. At last she reached the cave's opening. She passed the basket through and followed. Once outside, she breathed a huge sigh of relief. She rested on the grass for a few moments before heading back.

~   ~   ~

Kelly went quickly to the Pescas' house and to her bedroom, putting the basket under the bed.

"Is that you, Kelly?" asked Mrs. Pesca from the kitchen.

"Ahh...yeah, it's me...out in a second."

Kelly smoothed her wrap and hair on her way into the kitchen.

"Paroe says thanks for the mangoes and stuff."

"She is such a sweet girl," noted Mrs. Pesca.

"I thought I'd spend some time looking through those plant and fish books you gave me before school starts."

"Sounds like a good idea. Before you get started, though, could you help me pick some genips?"

"I guess so. What are genips?" asked Kelly.

"I'm surprised Jack hasn't shown you," said Mrs. Pesca. "He loves it when they're in season. He'll eat them just about all day. Guess they haven't been ripe enough yet. Let me just grab a basket from the kitchen and I'll show you. Wonderful little fruits, really."

Kelly hoped she wouldn't notice the missing containers.

Mrs. Pesca came out of the kitchen and headed out the arched door-way. Kelly breathed a sigh of relief and followed as she went around to the back of the house. Next to a shining white sculpture of a dolphin stood a tall tree. Its outer branches were full of round fruits about the size of small limes with light-green leathery skin.

"So, how are you at tree climbing?" questioned Mrs. Pesca.

"Okay, I guess," answered Kelly, looking up at the tree packed with the odd fruits. She had climbed a few trees back home and this one looked pretty easy, with lots of thick limbs to stand on—not like the coconut palms she'd seen some of the islanders shimmy up. No way she could do that.

"Make sure you stay on the thick branches and always hold on with one hand," instructed Mrs. Pesca. "The skinny branches with the bunches of genips on them break off pretty easy. Just toss them down and I'll put them in the basket."

Kelly didn't think it looked too hard, especially compared to the slippery cave, but she was tired from the climb up.

"Okay, here goes."

She grabbed a fat branch about shoulder height high, stepped into a v-shaped notch at the tree's base, and hoisted herself up. From there she climbed up from limb to limb. To get to the fruit, she'd have to climb out on one of the branches. She stopped to catch her breath. Normally it wouldn't have been hard, but she was already so tired. She looked down.

"That's it, you're doing great," coached Mrs. Pesca. "Okay, now just walk out on the branch to your right—see all of the bunches at the end there?"

Kelly decided looking down wasn't such a great idea. She carefully placed one foot after the other on the thick branch and looked for limbs to hold on to. Some were too skinny. Her legs were shaking as she moved farther out on the branch. The genips were almost in reach.

"You've got it now, Kelly. Steady yourself and break off that big bunch just above your left ear."

Kelly checked her balance, turned, and saw a bunch of the round green balls. She reached up with one hand. The branch snapped easily in her fingers.

"Here it comes," she shouted to Mrs. Pesca below. "Watch out, bombs away!"

Kelly dropped the bunch, but her aim was a bit off. The cluster of small balls plopped right on top of Mrs. Pesca's head and bounced off onto the ground.

"Sorry 'bout that," said Kelly sheepishly.

"Oh, no problem, dear…happens all the time," replied Mrs. Pesca, rubbing her head and putting the fruit into the basket.

Kelly took a deep breath and looked for more genips in reach. The next bunch she dropped thankfully landed right in the basket and soon it was overflowing.

"That's plenty, honey. Come on down."

Kelly carefully climbed down and was soon on the ground standing next to Mrs. Pesca. She was ready to collapse.

"Well now, let's check out the fruits of your labor," said Mrs. Pesca. "How about a seat in the shade next to this lovely dolphin?"

Kelly gladly sat down with Mrs. Pesca next to the sculpture.

Mrs. Pesca handed her a genip.

"Here's how you eat them," she instructed. "Just break open the skin with your fingers like this and pop the inside into your mouth. There's a large pit, so you just suck off the pulp."

With the fruit in her mouth, Mrs. Pesca looked like a kid eating a big round jawbreaker candy.

"These are nice and sweet. When they're not ripe, they can be quite tart."

Kelly split the genip as Mrs. Pesca had done and popped the inside into her mouth. She sucked on the pulp surrounding the large pit. Its texture was like the inside of a grape. It tasted delicious, sweet and kind of like a plum.

"Mmm, that's good," she mumbled. It was hard to talk with the fruit in her mouth.

Mrs. Pesca spit out the pit she had been sucking on and Kelly did the same. She handed Kelly a small bunch and popped another into her mouth.

"You fit in very well here, Kelly. I know Jack and his friends like having you around. And Mr. Pesca and I love having you here."

"Uh-huh, everyone's been really nice," replied Kelly smiling, sucking on the fruit.

"I know this is very hard. And we will never replace your family in the other world, but I hope you will come to love us like a new family. Dolphin Island is a wonderful place to live."

Kelly felt badly about not telling Mrs. Pesca the truth.

"I still want to go home, you know," she said.

"Of course you do," replied Mrs. Pesca compassionately. "We understand that. Did talking with Hank help?"

"Uh-huh, in a way."

Kelly really didn't want to talk about it.

"You know, I'm kind of tired," she said, yawning. "Is it okay if I go inside and lie down?"

"Oh sure, sure. You know if you ever want to talk, I'm here, anytime at all. We always wanted a sister for Jack. We just love having you here," said Mrs. Pesca, giving Kelly a big hug.

Kelly went into the house and to her room. She lay thankfully down on the bed. She felt bad and hoped the Pescas would understand if she got to go with Hank. They were very nice, but she already had a family and a home.

20

After dinner Kelly went to bed early, pretending to be exhausted. She had taken a nap that afternoon and wasn't tired at all, but she was too nervous and distracted to talk with Mr. and Mrs. Pesca, play a game with Jack, or read. She thought it would be better to spend some time alone, preparing herself for later. It would take all of her newfound bravery to sneak out of the house and make her way to where she was supposed to meet Hank.

~   ~   ~

Kelly waited as long as she could after Jack and his parents had gone to bed. She then grabbed the basket from under the bed, carefully opened her door, and peeked out. She wished that she didn't have to do this alone. If only she could tell Jack. She'd feel much better if he or Paroe was going with her. But there was no way around it; she was on her own.

The house was silent. A faint glow came from the living room, where all but one light orb had been put away. She tiptoed from her room. The tree in the living room made it kind of creepy at night. As quietly as possible, Kelly moved toward the door. Just then she heard rustling, the sound of someone moving. She dove behind the short wall separating the little kitchen area from the main room. Had she remembered to shut her bedroom door?

Kelly slowly peeked out from behind the wall, her heart racing. She saw Jack's back as he entered the bathroom. She froze in place, holding her breath. A few minutes later Jack walked out, yawning. He was staring straight ahead, nearly right at her. She ducked lower behind the wall. When she looked a few minutes later, he had gone back into his bedroom.

Kelly let out a huge breath, but stayed crouched behind the wall for another ten minutes or so, waiting for Jack to fall back asleep.

Picking up the basket, she noticed that the coiled shell glass had fallen over. It must have happened when she dove behind the wall. The seashell was empty and there were glowing drops and puddles in the basket and on the floor. She wiped up the floor, hoping she had enough of the algae water left in the coconut shell.

Kelly quietly opened the door of the Pescas' house and exited, shutting it carefully behind her. Luckily no one locked their doors on Dolphin Island, otherwise she'd have trouble getting back in. She tiptoed away from the house cautiously, watching out for Jack's land crab pal as well as the iguana, Fred.

There were scattered light orbs placed along the village's walkways. To be safe, Kelly stayed in the shadows and off the main path. She tried not to squash anyone's garden too badly. Her heart was beating rapidly and her hands were sticky with nervous sweat.

She stopped at the edge of the village where the path inland began. Without the walkway orbs lighting the way, the trail ahead was much darker. Kelly took a couple of deep breaths, willing herself to be calm and focused on the task at hand. She'd have to put aside any thoughts of creatures jumping out of the dark or of getting lost. She pulled the coconut shell container from the basket and removed its lid. Immediately, she was bathed in a blue glow from the sparkling water within. She held the makeshift flashlight in front of her to illuminate the way.

Kelly walked slowly, careful to keep the light on the trail. The path was fairly wide and well worn, so it wasn't too difficult to follow even at night. Soon she came to the narrow turnoff to the right and took it.

After passing the treehouse, she headed into the dark forest, definitely a more foreboding task. She hoped she remembered correctly the directions from Hank. She saw the red peeling bark of the large gumbo-limbo tree and turned north toward the salt flat.

Kelly mustered all of her courage and some she hadn't even known was there as she headed deeper into the forest. Around her the sounds of night on the island were loud. Crickets buzzed, a few birds squawked, and frogs croaked loudly. It was very still and she could hear the rustling of leaves when small lizards darted out of her way. Were there larger creatures lurking in the shadows just out of sight? She kept her eyes glued on the ground ahead, searching with the light. Where was it? Where was the marker? Had she already gone the wrong way? Her pulse raced, her heart thumping loudly in her chest.

Then she saw a glint of white off to the right. There it was—the first marker, a small seashell. And from there, up ahead, every so often, were more small seashells—just as Hank had promised. Kelly began following the trail of seashells through the dark woods.

At one point she tripped over a thick tree root and spilled some of the glowing water. Kelly kept on, trying not to think about the snakes, centipedes, or large land crabs that inhabited the woods—or whatever else might be out there. She just kept going, thinking about going home, about seeing her parents again, and about staying on the trail. Something larger scurried by on the ground in front of her. She let out a small shriek and ran ahead.

At last Kelly came to the salt flat. She was glad to be out of the forest. She held the glow from the coconut shell over an edge of the sand and its surface glistened like diamonds. She continued on, following Hank's directions and the seashell markers.

Soon she came to a mangrove forest; even at night it smelled like rotten eggs. Kelly climbed onto the thick roots of a mangrove tree. She'd have to climb from root to root to stay out of the mud and follow the trail. The blue glow over the crooked mangrove roots created eerie snake-like shadows that flickered across the muddy ground. Kelly hopped from root to root as fast as she could, trying to stay focused on each movement and not on the shadowy forms moving all around her. When she came to the edge of the mangroves, she jumped off the roots, landing in the sand of a small beach. She thought she heard something moving in the brush at the other end of the beach.

"Hello…Hank, is that you?"

There was no answer. She walked tentatively along the sand. Now she definitely heard rustling up ahead, but in the darkness she couldn't tell who or what it was.

"Hank, is that you?" she asked nervously.

A man stepped from the mangroves at the far end of the beach.

"Kelly, is that you?"

She let out a long sigh.

"Hi," she said breathlessly.

"Well now, I am impressed. I didn't really think you'd come."

Hank walked over to Kelly and put an arm around her shoulders.

"I see you've brought your own island flashlight. You are a resourceful young lady. Any trouble getting away unnoticed?"

"I don't think anyone heard me leave," replied Kelly. "Can they see us from the village?"

"No, I don't think so," said Hank. "It's a very dark night and we're pretty far away. Besides I'm hoping the island itself will block the view. The boat's over here in the mangroves. You can help shove us off."

Kelly followed Hank into the mangroves. A narrow stream flowed between the mangroves and a cliff on the other side. Sitting in the little creek was an odd-looking boat. Unlike the village canoes, which had a v-shaped hull, it had a flat bottom. There was also a long notch cut through the boat's floor at its center. A curved, smooth wooden board stuck up inside the boat through the notch.

"C'mon, help me push it out," said Hank. "The stream is pretty shallow right now, as the tide is just coming in."

Kelly put her coconut shell light on the bench seat in the front of the boat. She and Hank then waded through the stream, pushing the flat-bottomed boat out into the ocean. Within minutes the boat was floating in water up to their shins just off the beach.

"Okay, hop in," said Hank.

"Is there a paddle for me?" asked Kelly as she climbed in and sat at the bow.

"Oh sure. It's there behind you, under the middle seat."

Hank climbed in and Kelly picked up the paddle, putting her light into a small holder built into the side of the boat.

"Looks like a perfect fit," noted Hank. "Those holders will be for lights and things while we're paddling. Now let's go out a little ways where it's a bit deeper so I can put the centerboard down and see how it rides."

"Centerboard?" asked Kelly.

"It's this piece of wood, here at the floor. When the board is up, the boat has a flat bottom and shallow draft—meaning it can float in very shallow water, like over the reef, *I hope*. I can push the board through this slit in the bottom and it gives it more of a v-shaped hull like the village canoes, for better stability in the waves on the other side of the reef."

It was a calm night, with just a slight breeze blowing. Small ripples moved over the lagoon's surface. The tide would be especially high due to the phase of the moon—new. And with the new moon, there wouldn't be any moonlight, so it was also especially dark. It was a combination that Hank was counting on.

Kelly and Hank slowly paddled out into the lagoon. With each stroke through the water, the tips of their paddles lit up with blue-green sparks and the bow was bathed in a crest of shimmering light.

"It's just the bioluminescence," observed Hank. "The motion disrupts small creatures in the water and they give off light. They think you're a predator and this is their way of scaring you off or startling you. You'll get used to it."

Kelly wasn't so sure that she'd get used to it or that she even wanted to. She thought it was wonderful.

"Okay Kelly, that's deep enough. Let's get the centerboard down and see how she rides." Hank put his paddle down and shoved the board through the slit in the boat's hull.

"Looks pretty good," he said. "Let's paddle and see how she moves."

"Which way?" asked Kelly.

"Out toward the reef."

Kelly paddled in short smooth strokes as Trig had shown her. With the centerboard down, the boat was harder to steer straight, but after a while they got better at it.

"Hold on for a minute," said Hank. "We don't really need the centerboard back here in the lagoon. It's for out beyond the reef where the waves will be bigger." He pulled the centerboard back up into the boat.

Kelly stayed pretty quiet, following directions from Hank. She was focused on showing him that she could paddle well and be a big help when he left for real.

They headed farther out into the lagoon. The coconut shell light at the front and a small orb Hank had put in another holder about midway back lit the water around the boat. They could hear small waves breaking in the distance and could just make out a thin line of whitewater at the reef's crest.

Kelly leaned over the boat's side, but saw nothing in the dark water below.

"Let's head out to the reef," said Hank. "I'd like to see how deep the water is over the crest. Even with this flat bottom, we'll need some water over the top to get across."

"Okay," answered Kelly. "The boat seems pretty good."

"Well, at least it's not leaking."

They were approaching the back reef and could see a little bit of white foam spilling across the reef's shallow crest. Kelly didn't see how the boat could get across the reef—at its crest it looked to be only inches deep, even with the upcoming high tide.

"Let's go along the back reef and look for a sandy spot," said Hank. "I want to jump out and take a closer look at just how deep the water is over the crest. I'll paddle; you hold the light over the side and look for sand."

Kelly put her paddle down and held the coconut shell light over the side. Under its glare she could see through the clear water. They seemed to be in about two or three feet of water. The boat passed over some purple finger coral and a tangle of skinny coral branches.

"See any sandy spots?"

"Not yet," answered Kelly and she continued looking.

"There's a good spot coming up," she said a few minutes later.

Hank stopped paddling. As they glided forward, he hopped carefully out of the boat, landing in the sand.

"Hand me the line by your feet," said Hank, "and I'll tie us off."

Kelly hoped he did a better job than Angel had done the other day.

"Pass me the light orb from the boat. I'm going to check out the depth on the reef crest. You just sit tight, Kelly. I'll be back in a minute."

Kelly passed him the glowing orb and watched as he carefully weaved his way through the coral in a narrow channel of sand toward the reef's shallowest area. She held her coconut light over the side and looked into the water. At first she saw nothing but sand under its glare. Then tiny creatures began to flit back and forth. Soon small fish and shrimp darted among the moving specks. Kelly wondered if they were attracted to the light. She looked up and could see Hank in the distance nearing the line of whitewater at the reef's crest.

She stared back into the water, captivated by the bevy of tiny sea creatures now gathering under her light. Soon it became a frenzy of activity. Small fish shot through the water, feeding on the smaller animals. Kelly was glad she was sitting in the boat. She continued to watch as a growing number of fish came to feed at the unexpected smorgasbord under the light's glare. Suddenly, a small bright red missile shot through the water. Kelly jumped back. *What was that?*

She leaned over and put the light back at the water's surface. There it was again—*whoosh*. This time the creature came back and sat just at the edge of the light's illumination. Kelly recognized it from pictures she'd seen in a book. It was a small squid. It was red in color with skin that seemed translucent. The squid had a baglike body, large round eyes on either side of its small head, and long tentacles at its front. There were also thin fluttering fins along the length of its body. As Kelly stared at the creature, waves of color moved through the squid until it became nearly transparent, with only a slight tint and polka dots of red remaining. She was captivated by the creature. It too seemed curious, inching slowly into the light, gently waving its tentacles. She was so engrossed in watching the squid that she didn't notice Hank returning to the canoe or the dark triangular fin that was also silently moving toward the boat.

"Hey Kelly, whatcha see?" asked Hank as he carefully made his way back.

"I think it's a squid. How'd it look over the reef?"

"It's still pretty shallow," answered Hank worriedly. "We'll have maybe a foot or two of water if it's calm, but if the wind kicks up and the waves get any bigger, it's going to be dicey."

As Hank neared the boat, the black fin also came closer, unnoticed.

Kelly sat back, lifting the light away from the water. The glow from the coconut shell now reached a broader circle around the boat. She saw the fin.

"Look, Hank!" she shouted, pointing excitedly toward the fin. "Maybe it's Slash."

Hank looked in the direction she was pointing.

"Ahh, that's not a dolphin, Kelly. Move back so I can get in at the bow—that's a shark!"

Kelly scrambled back in the boat. But by then the shark was swimming at the boat's bow, just where Kelly had only moments ago been holding the light. It was moving between Hank and the boat.

Hank stood very, very still, watching the shark swim past. They both held their breath, waiting to see what it would do next. Kelly's curiosity got the better of her and she looked over the side to get a closer view.

The shark was about four feet long and swimming lazily at the surface. She watched as its tail swished from side to side and the shark's dark body bent in an S-shape, gliding smoothly, silently forward.

"Where is it?" asked Hank nervously.

"It's swimming at the back of the boat, coming around to the other side."

The boat had swung around, so Hank would have to climb over the sharp coral to get in on the side opposite the shark. Kelly looked at Hank and then at the shark, praying it wouldn't attack him.

Then Hank threw the light orb into the boat and dove toward it. The shark sensed the movement and swam toward him.

Hank grabbed the side of the boat, leapt onto the jagged coral, pushed off, and landed in the boat. As he jumped in, the shark bumped his leg. Then it swam slowly off into the darkness of the lagoon.

"Are you okay?" inquired Kelly. She looked down at his feet and saw blood seeping out of several gashes.

"It's just a few minor cuts from the coral," he said, sighing with relief. "*Phew,* that was a close one. I know they say here that sharks aren't a problem. But I still don't like 'em."

"Yeah, I know what you mean," agreed Kelly. "Though that one didn't attack you or anything. And to be honest, it looked kinda cool swimming by."

"Well, I gotta go back in to untie the line so we can head in," said Hank, eyeing the water around the boat warily.

Kelly looked at his bleeding feet.

"Doesn't blood attract sharks?" she asked with concern.

"I'll make it really quick," said Hank hesitantly.

"Can't we just cut the line?"

"I suppose," said Hank, "but I'd hate to leave it out on the reef. Some creature might swallow it or get tangled in it. It's a very easy knot. I'll be in and out in a second. You just hold the light over the side so I can see better."

Kelly couldn't believe what came out of her mouth next.

"Do you want me to do it?" she offered. "I'm not bleeding."

"Are you sure you want to?" asked Hank in surprise.

"You just said it was an easy knot," answered Kelly, not really feeling as confident as she was trying to sound.

"I don't see any more sharks around. But are you sure you want to go in?"

"I can do it," said Kelly, as much to herself as to Hank. She handed him the light, and before she could change her mind, Kelly hopped out of the boat. She swam quickly to where the line was tied to some rubble, ducked underwater, and opened her eyes. She undid the knot as fast as she could. Meanwhile, Hank nervously scanned the sea surface looking for the shark.

"C'mon Kelly, make it fast, time to go…"

As soon as the knot was undone, Kelly made for the boat. She didn't stop and look around, afraid of what she might see. When she was within reach of the boat, Hank quickly pulled her in.

"Well, now I'm even more impressed," said Hank, looking at Kelly with respect. "Let's head in. You've got to get back and I've got some work to do on the boat before tomorrow night."

Kelly couldn't believe what she had just done. She had faced her ultimate fear in the ocean—sharks. But the shark hadn't attacked, and actually she thought it had looked kind of graceful, peaceful even. Kelly wondered if sharks really deserved their reputation as people-eating monsters. She picked up a paddle and stroked proudly toward shore. In no time they were back at the creek between the mangroves and the cliff. They got out and pushed the boat into the small stream.

"Can you find your way back?" asked Hank.

"Definitely," responded Kelly immediately, now full of confidence.

Hank looked at her, contemplating his next words carefully.

"You know, you were a huge help tonight and are certainly a brave, resourceful young woman. If you still want to come tomorrow night, I'll talk to Pearl. But it's going to be very dangerous," he said.

"Oh yes, I want to come. I want to go home."

"There's no guarantee we'll get across the reef, and even if we do, you may get hurt and you still might not get home."

"I know, but I have to try," said Kelly with determination.

"Okay, meet us here at the same time tomorrow night. Again be very careful leaving. No one must know we are going."

"Thank you, oh thank you. I'll be here."

Kelly made her way back through the mangroves. The coconut shell was only about half full of glowing water due to spills. She'd have to get more of the algae water from the cave the next day. Without it, she'd never she'd find her way in the dark to meet Hank and Pearl. She definitely didn't want to risk missing them.

The walk home was slow and she was exhausted, but Kelly was so happy that Hank had said she could go that she no longer noticed the sounds, shadows, or even the movements in the forest that had frightened her earlier. She got back to the village and quietly crept into the Pescas' house. By the time she lay down, the sun was just peeking up over the horizon.

21

The next morning Kelly slept unusually late—even longer than Jack did.

"Well, Kelly, Jack's ways must be rubbing off on you," remarked Mrs. Pesca when she arrived for breakfast.

"She's finally seeing the light. Sleep is good," added Jack, rubbing his eyes.

"Guess I just needed to catch up a little," said Kelly groggily.

"It's your last day before school starts," said Mrs. Pesca. "What's on the agenda for the day?"

"Oh Mom, it's too early to think," replied Jack, yawning. "Can I just have some milk, some eggs, and *no papaya?* Maybe we'll go to iguana beach again. I think Kelly's beginning to like the iguanas."

"They're not so bad, I guess," said Kelly. "Iguana beach might be good. I'd love to see the dolphins again."

She still wished she could find a way to get Slash to show her the mysterious passage through the reef. At some point during the day, she'd also have to sneak away to the cave and get some more of the glowing algae water.

Jack and Kelly agreed on going to iguana beach. Kelly suggested they see if Paroe wanted to come along. If it was to be her last day on Dolphin Island, she wanted to spend it with Jack and Paroe, the new best friends she may never see again.

~   ~   ~

"Anyone home?" shouted Jack as they approached the open door to the Aguans' house.

Paroe came out looking very sad.

"What's the matter?" asked Kelly.

"It's my mom. She stayed over last night and was crying a lot. She's really upset about something."

"Maybe she just misses living with you and Skip," said Jack.

Of course, Kelly knew why Paroe's mother was so sad, but she couldn't say anything.

"You want to go to iguana beach?" asked Kelly. "Maybe it will cheer you up."

"I don't really feel like it," responded Paroe. "Skip has been storming around all morning. I should stay here with him."

"Oh come on. It's the last day before school starts," coaxed Jack.

"Yeah, it'll be fun," added Kelly.

"Well, maybe you're right. Okay, let me see if Skip will come with us."

Jack and Kelly waited outside. Kelly felt awful. Their departure that evening could mean that Paroe might never see her mother again.

Skip refused to come along, so the three of them headed south through the village toward the wetlands on the way to iguana beach. Just before reaching the swamp, they ran into the pudgy boy Ham, along with Trig and Angel. They were headed to a place Kelly hadn't visited yet, though she'd heard a lot about it—they called it *River Run*.

"You guys want to come?" asked Trig.

Kelly didn't know what to do. She wanted to find Slash again, even though she didn't know how to get the dolphin to show her the way through the reef.

Jack looked questioningly at Kelly.

"Well, make a decision already. Want to come or not?" said Angel brashly.

Now Paroe was looking at Kelly as well.

Finally Kelly nodded and they agreed to go. The six of them headed off through the wetland, but instead of taking the walkway to iguana beach, they took a trail going through the island's interior.

"River Run is nearly on the opposite side of the island," Jack told Kelly. "To get there we'll go past the cave where they grow the glowing algae and around the volcano."

Kelly prayed it wasn't anywhere near the creek where Hank had left his boat.

From the boardwalk they headed into the forest. Kelly thought it looked a lot less scary during the day. Angel was at the front, followed by Trig and Ham. Paroe, Jack, and Kelly were at the back.

The ground began to slope upward and the volcano loomed to their right. The trail ran along the base of the sleeping mountain. Just ahead the path forked. To the right it was wide and packed down from heavy foot traffic; to the left it was narrow and less well worn. Angel led, taking the path to the left.

"The other way goes to the algae cave," noted Jack, stopping at the fork in the trail. "We're not supposed to go there by ourselves."

"How come?" asked Kelly.

"The cave floor is slippery."

Don't I know it, thought Kelly.

"There've been a couple of accidents," continued Jack. "And the algae farmers are always afraid someone will get hurt or contaminate the pools."

Kelly paused for a moment, wondering if she had contaminated the pools the other day when she had taken some of the glowing water and, if so, if anyone had noticed.

"C'mon, you slowpokes," shouted Angel.

Jack and Kelly ran to catch up with the others.

"What happens if the pools get contaminated?" whispered Kelly to Jack.

"The algae die. They have to drain the pools and start growing the algae from scratch."

Kelly prayed she hadn't contaminated the pools. What if she had and they somehow traced it back to her? She didn't want anyone asking her any questions, especially today. They probably would have heard about it by now if the algae had died; she was just nervous about later.

While she walked behind the others, Kelly thought about the previous night. She had almost been caught when Jack had gotten up to go to the bathroom. She wished there was a way to prevent that from happening when she left tonight. Then she remembered the goats.

"Hey Paroe. Can I ask you a plant question?"

"Sure."

"Remember when Skip almost fed that plant to the goats and you said it would make them sleep?"

"Yeah, he was going to give them some *Dreamweed*."

"Do people here really use it to sleep better?"

"Uh-huh, it works great."

"I...I sometimes have nightmares about the storm and all and was wondering if it would help?" She hated deceiving Paroe.

"I know what you mean," said Paroe sympathetically. "I hate nightmares, used to dream about the animals on the island getting killed. And one time, I thought the volcano was going to erupt and didn't want to go to sleep and be buried in lava. My mom put some *Dreamweed* in my milk at dinner so I'd sleep okay."

"How much did she use?"

Paroe thought for a moment.

"I think just a small leaf or so crushed up."

"Is it easy to recognize?"

"Pretty much. I'll show you if we see any along the way."

In front of Paroe, Ham was breathing hard.

"Are we almost there?" he asked. Beads of sweat dotted his forehead and his face was turning bright red.

"Just around the bend," assured Trig. "Here, have some water." She handed him a gourd that had been strapped to her shoulders like a backpack. He took a cork out of the top and drank a big gulp.

"Anyone else want some?" asked Trig, passing it around.

In front, Angel stopped abruptly. Trig ran into him, and like a chain reaction, they all bumped into the person ahead.

"Watch it!" exclaimed Trig. "What'd you stop for?"

"Look in the...down there...there's a bunch of dolphins. They're never here," said Angel curiously.

Everyone crowded up beside Angel. In front of them lay a rocky point of land that stuck out into the ocean. On either side of the headland, there was a small beach and a semicircular bay. In the distance they could see the coral reef that encircled Dolphin Island. But in closer, just off the rocky point and running outside the two bays, was a series of long brown patch reefs. In between the patch reefs and the point of land was a winding light-blue channel of water. Five dolphins were swimming and leaping in the water's twisting path.

Jack ran down to the beach to the left of the rocky point.

"C'mon," he said excitedly. "This will be even better with the dolphins here."

Angel ran down to join Jack, while Trig, Paroe, and Ham followed with Kelly.

"It's really simple, Kelly," said Trig. "We can watch them go through once. See, you go in on this side, swim out a little ways, and then get pulled into the river. Well, it's not really a river. We just call it that. It's the channel of light-blue water running in between the reefs and the land. Don't try to swim against the current. Just float and be sure to watch where you're going. You don't want to run into any fire coral."

From the beach, Kelly watched as Jack and Angel swam out toward the patch reefs.

"Watch this, Kelly," shouted Jack.

A few strokes later Jack was picked up by a strong current. He was moving quickly with the flow of water and was soon gliding fast through twists and turns among the patch reefs. Kelly watched as he flew through a straight section and then made a sharp right, all the while staying in the light-blue channel of water. Eventually Jack landed in the bay on the other side of the headland. He swam to the beach and ran quickly up and across the point of land, back to where Kelly and the others were standing.

"See, isn't that cool?" said Jack. "It's running pretty good today. Got to go right past the dolphins too. C'mon, try it."

Angel was coming around for a second run as well and even he was smiling.

Kelly thought it looked like fun and joined in as they all waded into the water.

"What does fire coral look like?" she whispered to Paroe, who had stayed by her side and was pointing out where to go.

"It's kind of orangey brown, very smooth, and looks sort of like the peaks of a crown on top of the reef. Stay with me and I'll show you some."

"What happens if you hit it?"

"Stings like crazy."

As they swam farther out into the bay, the water's flow began to tug at their bodies. As the flow strengthened, they moved faster. Angel and Jack grabbed one another and did somersaults, horsing around in the swift flow. Trig and Ham were next and zoomed along, trying not to run into the two boys ahead. Paroe stayed with Kelly as she floated with the fast-moving water, warning her when she got too close to a reef or if it looked as though she might miss a turn. Just as they were entering a bend around one of the patch reefs, Paroe tapped Kelly and pointed to some fire coral. Kelly nodded and stayed clear of it.

It was like being on an amusement ride—Nature's own watery rollercoaster. She coasted along as the flow of water took her past one reef and then swept her through a sharp bend to the right. After a few more twists and turns and a straightaway, Kelly flew by the small school of dolphins also playing in the current. She and the others landed in the bay on the other side of the headland.

"That was great," said Kelly to Paroe as they walked back to the take-off beach. "And did you see? I think one of the dolphins was Slash!"

"Wanna go again?" asked Jack.

"Definitely," they both said with enthusiasm.

They all got in again and headed for the flowing light-blue channel of water. Once more they were swept away, gliding effortlessly in between the reefs and the land. Kelly got more daring and imitated Jack, doing a somersault as they floated along. When they came to where the dolphins were playing she tried to stop, but the current was too strong.

After landing, the group of teenagers hung out in the shallow water laughing and splashing. Kelly, Jack, and Paroe stayed together and watched the school of dolphins.

"I think the dolphins want to play," said Paroe.

And sure enough, the five dolphins leapt and dove their way over to them. Soon the animals were swimming nearby, turning on their sides and looking curiously at each of them. Paroe put out her hand and was the first to be taken for a ride, then Jack, then Trig. Kelly held out her hand. Within seconds a dolphin came by, put its fin in her hand, and swept her off her feet. It was Slash, and once again she was flying through the water under dolphin power. The graceful creature zoomed along the surface, pulling her as if she weighed nothing at all. She forgot about everything but the feeling of coasting through the water beside the dolphin. This time it took her for a longer ride out toward the reef. She thought, *maybe it knows...maybe it will show me the way through.* But then Slash turned around and brought her back to the others.

The dolphins stayed with them for another hour, playing and taking them all for rides.

Afterward, when they were back on the beach, even Paroe seemed surprised. "I've never seen the dolphins *here*," she said.

"And they stayed so long. Ham, even you got a good ride," said Jack, whispering to Kelly, "He usually has trouble holding on."

"My best ever," said Ham with a huge grin on his face.

Even Angel was still smiling.

Kelly wondered if the dolphins somehow knew that she was planning to leave that night. Maybe it was a good omen or a going-away present.

"I'm starved. Let's head back," said Jack. "I could eat a *manatee*."

"Ugh, how can you even say that?" snapped Paroe, grimacing.

"Oh lighten up. It's just a joke. You're *soooo* sensitive," barked Angel.

Trig gave her brother a withering stare, while Paroe simply ignored him. They then headed to the trail leading back to the village.

On the way home they passed the main entrance to the algae cave, and it reminded Kelly of the things she still needed to do before nightfall.

"Hey Paroe, have you seen any of that *Dreamweed* around here?" she asked quietly.

"Oops, I almost forgot. You can always have some from what we have at the house."

About five minutes later, however, Paroe stopped and pointed to a skinny green plant with small round leaves growing in clusters of four.

"That's it right there," she said. "Here, one of these might help." She broke off two leaves and handed them to Kelly.

"Thanks," said Kelly taking the leaves. She looked at the girl walking beside her. She wished she could tell Paroe about what she was going to do later that night. She felt awful keeping it from her. And a part of her wished that she wasn't leaving Dolphin Island at all, leaving her new friends.

When the group reached the village, they split up as each went to their respective homes. Kelly said good-bye to everyone, not knowing if she would ever see any of them again. She felt especially bad about saying farewell to Paroe.

22

By the time they got back, made lunch, and ate, it was already mid-afternoon. Kelly still had to find a way to sneak out to the algae cave to get some more glow water, but both Jack and Mrs. Pesca seemed to be hovering around her. She was also worried because Paroe had given her only two *Dreamweed* leaves. She wasn't sure if it would be enough for Mr. Pesca, Mrs. Pesca, and Jack. She definitely didn't want to give them too much, but if she gave them too little, they might not be sound asleep when she tried to sneak out of the house. If she could find a way to go alone to the algae cave, maybe she could also find another *Dreamweed* plant. Kelly also had to figure out how to put the crushed leaves into their drinks at dinner without anyone noticing.

"I think I'll take a short nap," said Kelly.

"Are you feeling all right?" asked Mrs. Pesca.

"Yeah, I'm fine, just kinda tired."

Kelly thought Jack was looking at her a little suspiciously.

She stayed in her room for over an hour, trying to nap. But it was no use; she was too nervous.

She peeked out of her bedroom to see where Jack and his mother were. She didn't see either of them—maybe she could slip out without anyone noticing. She stepped into the living room.

"There you are," said Jack. "I was beginning to wonder what happened to you." He had been sitting at the table around the corner, paging quietly through a book.

"Want to go over some fish before school tomorrow?" he asked.

"Thanks, but I thought I'd go down to the beach before it gets dark out," said Kelly, thinking what a lame excuse it was to get out of the house.

"Great idea, I'll come."

Kelly groaned silently, wondering if she could make do with what was left in the coconut shell. Then another idea came to her.

"Before we go, I've been wondering. How do they fill the orbs with the glowing algae water?"

"Oh, that's easy," responded Jack, taking an orb from a covered basket at the base of the tree in the living room. "See, when you turn it over—it's this spot on the bottom. They tie it and then put some glue over the knot so that it doesn't leak and so it stands up better. To refill it, you cut off the glue and untie it."

"Hmmm, that does seem easy," noted Kelly. "You want to get some genips before going to the beach?"

Jack eagerly agreed and the two of them picked a bunch of genips from the tree out back and walked to the beach. They sat on the sand, sucking on genips and looking out over the lagoon. Some of the villagers were just paddling in after a day out on the water; others were putting the boats away for the night. There was also a group of young children building a giant sandcastle nearby.

"You know, I think the water here is the prettiest color I've ever seen," observed Kelly. "It doesn't look like this where I come from."

"I wonder why?" pondered Jack.

Kelly thought about it for a moment.

"Maybe it's because of pollution," she said sadly. "I guess we don't treat the ocean or its animals as well as you do here."

"Doesn't make sense not to, to me," said Jack simply. "We live off the ocean and swim in it, and besides we love the dolphins and other things that live there—why wouldn't we take care of it and be thankful for it?"

"Seems pretty stupid, doesn't it?" said Kelly. "How come it's called Dolphin Island?"

"I think it's because the dolphins help us and have always helped us. They're part of the history of the island. Some say that the people who first came here were brought by dolphins, just like you."

"Really?"

"Yeah, others think that's just a myth."

"Where I come from there's a place called the Bermuda Triangle that's supposed to be very mysterious, though some people think it's just a myth too. There are stories about boats and planes that went into it and disappeared. Funny thing is that we were sailing in the Bermuda Triangle when I fell off the boat and ended up here. I wonder if they're connected somehow."

"I don't know. It would be kind of cool if you could go back and forth," said Jack.

"Do you want to see what it's like outside the island?"

"I guess so. I've heard about some of the things you have there, like cars and those computer things—they sound cool. But I'd hate not being able to come back. Besides, people say that if you could come and go from this island like in your world and more people knew about it, Dolphin Island would be ruined."

"Yeah, you're probably right," sighed Kelly.

"Do you miss it a lot?"

"I miss my parents and even my older brother, Thomas, though he could be a real pain. Don't get me wrong. You and your mom and dad have been really great…but I still want to go home."

"Maybe someday someone will figure out how to get safely through the reef and you could go," said Jack kindly.

"Maybe, and then you could come and stay with me and my family for a while."

"Only if I could come back," said Jack. "So what's it really like anyway?"

Kelly thought about telling Jack all about Massachusetts, her friends, and her family back home, but she didn't really want to talk about it, afraid she might let something slip about the plan for later that night. And besides it was starting to get dark and she still had to somehow get the *Dreamweed* into the glasses before dinner.

"I'm starved. Let's head back," said Kelly, trying to change the subject. "Wonder what we're having for dinner?"

Jack seemed to understand that she didn't want to talk about her family or home. On the short walk back, in his usual fast-paced mode, he listed all the different things they could be having for dinner and which he preferred.

Then, just as they approached the Pescas' home, Jack stopped abruptly.

"This is it," he whispered. "That crab is mine."

He began slowly stalking the clawed creature that now sat a short distance from its hole by the side of the house, as if teasing Jack—*Look... ha-ha...I'm out in the open and you can't get me.*

Jack was about four feet from the land crab and still it didn't move. He inched closer. Soon he was just two feet away.

Kelly began to think that maybe this time he really would catch the crab. Jack crept closer and the crab inched toward its burrow. He moved back and the crab came out a step.

Jack then turned his back on the crab as if he wasn't interested anymore, and the crab came further away from its hole.

Suddenly, Jack wheeled around, diving for the crab. He'd caught it!

"*YOUCH!*" yelled Jack as the crab dug one of its large claws into his hand. He immediately released his grip on the creature and it quickly scurried into its burrow.

"*AARGH!*" shouted Jack, pounding his fist on the ground in frustration.

The crab sat in its hole looking out and Kelly swore it was smiling. She really would miss Jack—hopefully.

23

Just before dinner Kelly went into the kitchen. In her room she had crushed the two leaves Paroe had given her and now had the powder in a small pouch tucked into one of the folds of the two-piece blue-and-white wrap she wore.

"Can I help with anything?" asked Kelly, trying to sound very innocent.

"Sure, you can set the table," said Mrs. Pesca. "It's usually Jack's job, but I'm sure he won't mind. And besides, we'll have to start splitting up some of the chores around here now that you've settled in a bit."

"Okay," said Kelly, grabbing four scallop shell plates and the conch shell silverware. She also took four of the coiled shell glasses from the shelf above the sink. She brought everything out to the table and set out each place setting.

"Do you want me to pour the drinks?" she asked, thinking this could be easier than she thought.

"No thanks, I'll get it," replied Mrs. Pesca. "Why don't you come in here and stir the pot a bit. I'll get the water."

Kelly had to act fast. Jack was nowhere to be seen and Mrs. Pesca was still in the kitchen, just out of sight. She took out the pouch of crushed *Dreamweed* and poured equal amounts into the cups in front of where Mr. Pesca, Mrs. Pesca, and Jack usually sat. She hoped it would be enough and prayed that Mrs. Pesca wouldn't notice.

Kelly went into the kitchen just as Mrs. Pesca was coming out. Her hands were shaking. She tried to think of a way to distract Jack's mother so she wouldn't see the green powder in the bottom of each glass as she poured.

"What's for dinner?" she asked, leaning around the short wall to watch Mrs. Pesca filling the glasses. The woman turned to her while pouring.

"It's conch chowder with a little fish and some vegetables thrown in."

So far so good—two of the glasses were filled and she hadn't noticed. Kelly hoped there was enough *Dreamweed* in each. Then trouble struck.

"Oh my, look at the dirt in this glass," noted Mrs. Pesca as she picked up one of the glasses and brought it into the kitchen. She rinsed it and then refilled the glass with water. Kelly came out of the kitchen area. Mrs. Pesca had just put the glass down in front of Jack's seat.

Minutes later Mr. Pesca arrived home and Jack came to the table. There was nothing else she could do. She'd just have to take her chances later and hope that Jack would stay asleep this time.

They all sat down at the table for dinner. Kelly barely made it through the meal without bursting. Every time Mr. or Mrs. Pesca took a sip of water, she wondered if they would taste the *Dreamweed*. Dinner seemed to go on forever, but finally they were done and the plates were cleared and washed.

Kelly wished she could just say good-bye to the Pescas and go into her room until it was time to leave. Instead she stayed for an agonizing two hours playing a game of cards with the family. Finally, Mr. and

Mrs. Pesca began to get sleepy and headed for bed. Kelly wondered if it was the *Dreamweed*. She gave them each a big hug and said goodnight, thinking *good-bye* and *thank you*.

"I'm pretty beat," said Kelly to Jack. "I think I'll go to bed too." She then gave him a hug as well.

"Ahhh, okay, whatever," said Jack, stunned by her display of affection. "See you in the morning."

Kelly thought he was looking at her oddly—maybe he knew. No, there was no way. It was just her nerves.

Kelly went into her room, hoping Jack would go to bed soon. In the meantime, she collected a few of the wraps and seashells she planned to take and the coconut shell container half-filled with glow water. On a sheet of paper from a pad in her room—decorated with jumping dolphins, of course—she wrote the Pescas a note thanking them and saying good-bye. Then she lay down on the bed and waited anxiously.

~ ~ ~

After about two hours Kelly thought it might be safe to go; besides she was going crazy in the small bedroom. She left the note on her bed, inched open her door, and looked into the hallway. The Pescas' bedroom door was closed and Jack's room was quiet. She prayed the *Dreamweed* would keep Mr. and Mrs. Pesca sound asleep, and she just had to hope that Jack wouldn't wake up. Kelly took one last, fond look around the small bedroom and crept as quietly as possible into the living room.

In the dim light of the one orb left out, she went to the basket sitting under the tree. She removed an orb, covering it with one of her extra wraps, and tiptoed into the kitchen. She put the orb on the stone counter and took out her coconut shell light, placing it next to the orb and removing the lid. Light filled the small kitchen area. Quickly, she looked around for something to dim the glow. Finding a small cloth for drying dishes, she threw it over the coconut shell.

Kelly needed something to cut the ties or at least poke a hole in the orb. She looked through the utensils in a large shell holder for something suitable—they rattled slightly. She found a small knife. Should she poke a hole in the orb or cut through the string and glue holding it together? She was about to poke a small hole just below the string when she thought she heard a noise somewhere in the house. She stayed very still and listened. Was it real or just her imagination? The house was silent. She looked back at the orb and poked a small hole just beneath the glue and string. A tiny stream of glowing water shot into the air. Startled, Kelly dropped the knife, which fell to the floor with a loud *thwack.* She stood very still.

When she was sure that there were no sounds coming from either of the bedrooms, Kelly picked the knife up off the floor and carefully poured the glowing water from the orb into the coconut shell. She drained what was left in the orb down the sink and put the empty egg sack into her basket. She quietly cleaned the knife and wiped off the glowing water that had spilled onto the counter and floor. She needed to get going. Again she stopped and listened, thinking she had heard some rustling noises. Nothing.

Kelly took a deep breath, looked around the house one last time, and silently said a final good-bye to the family that had taken her in and been so kind. She thought one more time of her friends, Jack and Paroe. She'd miss Jack's antics, like chasing crabs and how he pretended to be so tough and made her laugh. She'd miss Paroe's kindness and her special way with animals. But mostly she'd miss having them at her side on adventures while exploring Dolphin Island. She then crept quietly out the door.

Like the night before, Kelly worked her way through the village, staying in the shadows. She had an uncomfortable feeling this time, as if someone or something was watching her. But when she looked around, she saw only gardens and the sea creature statues made of stone. She kept going. Kelly arrived at the treehouse, walked past the gumbo-limbo tree, and entered the forest. As before, she used the coconut shell light to follow the trail of small seashells through the woods toward the salt flat. She moved quickly, confident in herself and the trail. She barely noticed the sounds of crickets buzzing or the leaves rustling as small animals scurried by. But just before she reached the salt flat, she thought she heard something larger move in the forest behind her. She stopped and stayed very still. Only the natural sounds of night on the island could be heard.

Kelly went on, reaching the mangroves. She carefully put the coconut light in her basket, wedging it in by the extra wraps inside so that it would stand up. She needed a free hand to climb through the mangroves' tangled roots. Even the eerie snake-like shadows did little to slow her down this time. She made her way quickly toward the small beach. Again she thought she heard a sound behind her and turned around. This time she could swear she saw something large move in the dark. She hurried toward the beach.

Hopping off the mangroves, Kelly ran on the sand.

"Hank, are you here? It's me, Kelly," she said nervously, out of breath.

Hank stepped through the trees.

"You made it, great."

But Kelly didn't think Hank looked as excited as he was trying to sound. In fact, he appeared rather upset.

"What's the matter, Hank? You haven't changed your mind, have you? About me coming and all."

He turned back toward the mangroves where his boat was hidden and looked down.

"It's Pearl," he said. "I'm not sure she can do this."

Kelly followed Hank through the mangroves to where the boat sat in the little creek. Paroe's mother, Pearl, was sitting on the side of the canoe, her head in her hands, sobbing.

Hank put his arm around Pearl.

"They'll be fine. Their father loves them, and the rest of the village will take good care of them."

She looked up at Kelly. Her eyes were red and swollen.

"Hello Kelly," she said sadly. "I know, Hank, but they're my babies. I should be the one to look after them and see them grow up. Paroe needs a mother—she's a sensitive child, blessed with so many gifts. And Skip—he's so angry and sad, and it's my fault."

Kelly felt as if she was intruding, so she stepped back into the shadows while Hank and Pearl talked. She was about to sit down, when suddenly a hand clamped down on her shoulder.

Kelly stumbled and fell backward, landing on the person behind her. They both tumbled into the sand. Once their limbs were untangled, she realized who it was.

"Jack, what are you doing here?" said Kelly angrily, getting to her feet.

"I heard you leave and followed. What are you doing here?" he snapped back.

"I...I...I'm going to leave the island with Hank and Paroe's mother."

"You're what? How are you going to get through the reef? Are you crazy! You'll get killed. That's nuts. You can't go."

"Jack, you can't tell me what to do," retorted Kelly firmly, with her hands on her hips. "I don't belong here. I need to be with my family. I'm going. Hank's built a special boat."

"Kelly, lots of people have built special boats," said Jack, shaking his head. "They never work." In a softer tone he said, "Stay here with us, with me and my family."

"You've been great, really," said Kelly more calmly. "But I have to do this. I have to at least try to get back to my family."

"What's going on over there?" yelled Hank. "Who's there with you, Kelly?"

Kelly and Jack walked out of the shadows to where Hank and Pearl were standing next to the boat.

"Jack, what are you doing here?" asked Hank, annoyed.

"You can't leave. It's too dangerous."

"Jack, I appreciate your concern and all, but we're leaving and that's all there is to it."

Jack looked at Pearl.

"You're leaving too? What about Skip and Paroe? How can you abandon them? You can't just leave them."

Pearl took a big breath, looked at Hank, and then walked over to Jack and kneeled down in front of him.

"For such a young man, you are wiser than your age. That's just what we were discussing," she said, turning to Hank. "I can't leave my kids. I'm not going. I'm so sorry, Hank. You know I love you, but I can't leave. I just can't."

Hank looked miserable.

"I love you too, but I do understand," he said, walking over to Pearl and embracing her tightly.

Kelly felt awful for Hank, but at the same time she was happy for Paroe. She was glad Pearl had decided not to go and would remain on Dolphin Island with her kids. She just hoped it didn't mean that Hank would stay as well.

Hank reluctantly let go of Pearl and stepped back.

"Okay, the tide is rising and we want to hit it right at high," he stated, trying his best to sound enthusiastic. "We'd better get going. Kelly, it's just you and me then."

"But…but…," stammered Jack.

Kelly hugged him.

"Thank you for everything. You've been like a brother, but I have to do this. Say good-bye to your parents for me and to Paroe. Who knows, maybe one day we'll see each other again somehow. I'd really like that."

"Me too," said Jack glumly. "Well…ahh…make sure you look for a low spot on the reef, be careful paddling, watch the waves, and—"

"Good-bye, Jack," interrupted Kelly as she gave him another hug.

"Bye, Kelly."

Kelly put her basket in the boat, which was now stocked with water, food, a few orbs, a sail, extra paddles, a fishing rod, two orange-and-white square cushions, and some other equipment that had come from the wreckage of Hank's airplane.

Together, Hank, Pearl, Kelly, and Jack pushed the boat through the stream out into the ocean. At the beach, they all hugged again, Pearl and Hank the longest.

Hank and Kelly then pushed the boat out into knee-deep water and climbed in.

"I love you and will never forget you," yelled Pearl.

"Bye, Kelly...good luck," shouted Jack.

Hank and Kelly waved.

Hank then handed Kelly a flat yellow vest with black straps.

"Put this on...they were in my plane," said Hank, putting one on also. "It's a life vest. It goes on over your head like this and the strap wraps around you and hooks on."

Kelly put on the life vest.

"If you go in the water, pull the strap here and it should inflate—I hope," said Hank. Then they picked up their paddles and turned the boat toward the reef.

"Okay, this is it Kelly...we're off. Are you ready? Last chance to back out," said Hank.

"Let's go," replied Kelly more confidently than she felt.

"I've been surveying the reef for weeks. I think the lowest spot and best place to go over is just to the south of here," noted Hank. "Here, I split one of the larger orbs in two. Take this smaller one and put it up front."

He passed her a light orb about the size of a large orange. Kelly placed it in the holder at the bow of the boat and they started paddling for the coral reef that encircled Dolphin Island.

It was a clear, breezy evening. With the new moon it was very dark and the tide was indeed one of the highest of the year. But already they could hear the sound of waves breaking on the reef. It was not a comforting sound and Kelly's stomach constricted with fear. Going over the reef crest was scary enough, but with waves breaking on it, it was much more frightening.

Halfway through the lagoon, Kelly and Hank looked back toward shore. Pearl and Jack were standing on the beach, waving in the glow of a light orb. They waved back and continued paddling.

As they got closer to the reef, the sound of waves crashing on the crest grew louder. Kelly's grip on the paddle grew tighter. Even in the darkness she could see a thick line of whitewater at the reef.

Soon they were in the deceptively calm waters of the back reef, but up ahead some twenty-five feet lay the true nature of the task ahead. Waves, definitely bigger than the night before, were breaking at the shallowest point over the reef.

"See that spot up ahead?" said Hank, pointing. "Where there seems to be less whitewater over the reef?"

"I'm not sure," Kelly responded nervously, squinting toward the reef and the waves crashing at its crest.

"Let's go a little closer to get a better look and see what the depth is. I'll paddle, you look over the side with the light." He pushed them a little closer to the reef crest.

"Looks okay, maybe two feet," said Kelly, peering over the side.

"All right, I want you to paddle with me. Even if you get scared, keep paddling. If you lose the paddle, then hold on tightly. Are you ready, Kelly?"

"Yes, I'm ready," she answered, but in truth she was terrified. She gripped the paddle fiercely and gritted her teeth.

"Okay, let's do it...*Here we go!*" yelled Hank.

Kelly and Hank paddled hard. But after only a few minutes, before they had even reached where the waves were breaking, they felt a strong bump and the boat stopped abruptly.

Water and foam from the waves crashing ahead of them surged around the boat, splashing into it.

"We're stuck," shouted Hank. "Paddle backward."

They both tried to back-paddle, but nothing happened. The boat was hard aground on the coral.

"I'll have to get out and push us off," yelled Hank. "We'll have to find another way across."

"What about your feet?" shouted Kelly.

As he climbed out of the boat, Hank pointed toward his feet. He had on worn-out sneakers covered with lots of odd-shaped patches and gobs of dried glue.

"Had these on when I came to the island. Thought they would be fitting attire for when I left."

Kelly held on as Hank pushed and shoved, trying to get the boat off the coral. It took ten minutes of hard work, but finally he was able to get them floating, back in the calmer waters behind the reef.

He hoisted himself back in.

"See any holes?"

She looked at the floor of the boat. There didn't seem to be any water coming in.

"Nope."

"Okay, let's look for another place to cross."

24

Hank and Kelly paddled the boat along the back reef, searching for a spot where the waves were lower and the water was deeper.

"We don't have much time," urged Hank. "The tide will start going out and the water will get even shallower over the reef. Look for a spot that looks a little calmer."

Kelly scanned the reef ahead, but it all looked pretty much the same to her—waves crashing and white foam. And in the dark it was difficult to judge the water depth.

They continued paddling, following the reef as it bent around the island.

"We're just going to have to pick a place and go for it," said Hank. "How about up ahead...looks a bit better there."

They stopped paddling and let the boat coast to a stop. With a few strokes, Hank turned them toward the reef crest and hopefully, the open ocean beyond.

"Let me make sure the centerboard is up as high as it can go," said Hank, pulling up on the board in the middle of the boat. "It's not coming up any further. Okay then, that's it. Ready, Kelly?"

"I guess so."

Her resolve to be brave was beginning to falter. She was losing her nerve and beginning to think that Jack was right. Maybe it was crazy to attempt crossing the reef.

"*Let's do it!*" shouted Hank.

Kelly decided it was better just not to think about it. Besides it was too late to change her mind now. She took a deep breath and put her paddle in the water, and again they headed over the dangerous reef.

The boat had moved only a few feet when they felt a distinct bump at the bow. Kelly stopped paddling, assuming they had run up onto the coral again. There was another *THUMP* at the bow and the boat turned to the left. Kelly looked over the side, but didn't see anything in the darkness.

They definitely weren't aground, as the boat was still moving. However, instead of heading straight across the reef, they were now gliding slowly alongside it. Hank stopped paddling. Again, they felt a *THUMP* at the bow.

"Are we hitting coral? Do you see anything, Kelly?"

Kelly picked up a light orb and leaned over the side of the boat to look more closely. The boat tipped and she nearly fell overboard. As she caught her balance, Kelly found herself staring straight into a big, dark eye. Startled, she jumped backward, speechless.

"What is it?" asked Hank anxiously.

Kelly cautiously looked back over the side of the boat. This time when she saw the eye, a wide grin spread across her face.

"It's Slash, Hank. It's Slash."

There floating beside the bow of the boat was a dolphin. Its scarred head was tilted slightly to the side and the dolphin was looking directly at Kelly, almost knowingly.

Hank looked over the side and couldn't believe his eyes. There at the side of the boat was indeed a dolphin pushing at the bow with its beak, like a tugboat guiding a large ship.

The dolphin picked up its head and gave two loud squeaks.

"I think he's trying to tell us something," said Kelly, wishing Paroe was with them.

"What do you think it means?" asked Hank, shaking his head in amazement.

"I don't know. Maybe it doesn't want us to leave or go over the reef."

Just then they felt another bump, this time at the back of the boat, and they glided slowly forward.

"Hey, there's another dolphin back here," said Hank.

As the dolphin in back pushed the boat forward, Slash nudged the front to the left. After another push from the back, Slash swam to the other side of the boat and pushed them to the right. Soon they were slowly weaving their way not directly across the reef, but more alongside and diagonally across it. The dolphins were pushing and steering the boat through a winding channel in the coral on top of the reef.

Hank paddled gently to help the dolphins, while Kelly watched in front. Ever so slowly they made their way through twists and turns with the dolphins guiding the boat. Soon there was whitewater and foam all around the boat and it began to rock from side to side—they were over the reef crest. Kelly held tightly onto the sides. They felt a brief bump as the boat scraped the bottom. Hank paddled a little harder to combat the surging water all around them. And the dolphins kept at it…a push…a nudge…a push…a nudge.

Suddenly, both dolphins gave them a great shove from behind. The water around them turned dark and deep—they were past the reef. They had made it across. Kelly breathed a huge sigh of relief and picked up her paddle. She and Hank both stroked strongly, making their way out into the open ocean, away from the reef and away from Dolphin Island. Swimming nearby, the dolphins seemed to be watching their progress. The waves were no longer breaking; they were now two to three-foot-high passing hills. The flat-bottom boat began to roll and they had trouble steering.

"Keep paddling, Kelly. I need to put the centerboard down," said Hank.

He pushed hard on the centerboard so that it would drop through the slit in the boat's floor. Nothing happened. He tried again…it didn't move. Hank moved over the centerboard, trying to use his weight to push it down, but still it didn't budge.

"It must have gotten wedged in when we went up on the coral," said Hank anxiously. "I can't get it down."

"What should we do?" asked Kelly.

"We can either head back and try to get back in over the reef…or keep going and try to stay upright. But if the waves get any bigger, we'll be in trouble."

They both looked back the way they had come, considering what to do.

"Where's the reef?" questioned Kelly, surprised that she couldn't see the waves breaking over the coral that surrounded Dolphin Island.

"I don't know," replied Hank curiously. "We shouldn't be that far away yet…we should still be able to see it. That's strange."

Now, Hank was a good architect when it came to houses and buildings. But when it came to boats and the ocean, he was a novice. Without the centerboard and even with it, his boat design was fairly unstable in waves much higher than two feet. While they were looking for the reef and deciding what to do, a four-foot wave rolled toward them.

"*Uh-oh,* hold on, Kelly," yelled Hank as he felt the boat rise on the approaching hill of water.

The small boat rolled dangerously, but thankfully it stayed upright. However, the boat was now turned so that it sat in a precarious position, with its side facing into the oncoming waves.

Hank paddled desperately, trying to turn the boat's bow back into the waves. But they were still sitting sideways when the next wave struck. The boat tipped steeply and then, it flipped. Kelly screamed as both she and Hank were catapulted into the sea.

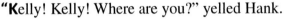

25

"Kelly! Kelly! Where are you?" yelled Hank.

"I'm over here," she shouted.

Hank swam over to her.

"Inflate your vest."

She pulled on the strap as he had shown her and air rushed into the yellow vest. Hank did the same thing. The boat was nowhere to be seen. Floating nearby were some of their supplies.

"Grab a cushion and anything else you can hold on to," urged Hank. They each grabbed an orange-and-white square cushion. Kelly floated on hers, while Hank put a gourd with water on his, as well as a few pouches of food and one of the small light orbs that had been floating nearby. They let a paddle drift away. It was of no use now.

"Now what?" asked Kelly, thinking, *not this again.*

"I'm *so* sorry, Kelly. I should never have let you come."

"No, I wanted to come," she said. "Maybe the dolphins will take us back."

"That would be *very good,*" replied Hank.

The dolphins had been nearby just before they capsized, but now they were nowhere to be seen. Kelly tried calling out to Slash. She even tried making squeaking and clicking noises, but she and Hank remained alone floating in the dark rolling waves.

Kelly remembered that Jack had said there were more sharks on the outside of the reef. Now she really hoped that sharks weren't the people-eating monsters so often portrayed. She treaded water and spun around looking for the dolphins, hoping she wouldn't see the triangular fin of a shark.

The minutes passed, and Kelly and Hank remained alone in the dark sea. Then Kelly thought she heard a familiar sound.

"Slash, is that you?"

Out of the darkness, a sparkling glow came toward them. This time Kelly knew what it was and wasn't frightened. Two dolphins swam out of the shimmering light and one came over to Kelly. The dolphin nuzzled her with its beak. She took one hand off the cushion to rub it. The animal with its telltale scar turned on its side and looked at her. Then with a nod of his head and a flick of the tail, Slash swam off. The other dolphin followed. They leapt into the air, twirled, and then dove deep and were gone from sight. Only a faint blue-green glow was left behind.

"Come back," shouted Kelly. "Show us the way back to the island."

The dolphins didn't return and the two of them floated silently.

After a while Hank put a hand on Kelly's shoulder.

"I'm really sorry," he said. "Looks like they're not going to help us this time. I think we're on our own."

Kelly couldn't believe it. Why wouldn't the dolphins bring them back to the island? She was sure Slash would help, just as he had before.

"When it gets light out, maybe there'll be a ship or another island," said Hank, trying to sound reassuring.

They drifted for several hours before the sun came up. Both he and Kelly took short naps. The life vests kept their heads above water even while they slept, but by dawn they were both exhausted and shivering.

The water was soaking the warmth and life out of their bodies. Kelly was scared, but even worse, she felt deserted by the dolphins. Why would they leave her now?

As the sun rose, they scanned the horizon, looking for the island, a ship, or the dolphins. But they saw nothing.

Kelly looked at Hank. He had stubble on his chin and his lips were cracked from being in the seawater. And he kept looking at her sadly.

They each took a few sips of water from the gourd they had recovered and ate some soggy fish from one of the rescued pouches. The sun rose higher in the sky.

"You are the bravest young woman I've ever met," said Hank. "Your parents would be very proud of you."

Kelly smiled.

Then Hank cocked his head to the side, listening.

"Do you hear the dolphins again?" asked Kelly hopefully.

"Not the dolphins, something else," replied Hank. "Quiet…listen."

Kelly stayed very still and listened. It was very faint, but she did hear something—a deep thumping sound.

"Is it a ship?" she asked.

"I don't think so," answered Hank, scanning the horizon.

They both turned in circles, searching for what was making the noise. They couldn't tell what it was or which direction it was coming from.

"There, look," shouted Kelly, pointing up into the sky at a black speck getting larger.

"I think it's a helicopter," said Hank excitedly, turning over the cushion he had been holding on to. Underneath, strapped on with silver duct tape, was a waterproof flare from his crashed airplane.

"Hope this still has some juice left in it."

Kelly's heart raced. Was it really a helicopter? Would they see them? She waved frantically as it got closer.

"Down here! We're down here!"

Hank pulled the tab on the flare and it let off a stream of red smoke. He held it up high over his head. The wind took the smoke, streaming it up and across the sky. In the morning sun, the red smoke was bright against the blue sky. Kelly crossed her fingers and prayed they'd see it.

The helicopter turned away and their hearts sank. But then it turned again, and this time it began heading straight toward them. As it came closer, the beating of its blades grew louder. Soon the helicopter was hovering directly overhead. The water around them was whipped up by the wind from its rotating blades.

Kelly flung herself on Hank.

"We're saved!" she shouted joyfully. "We're going home!"

"Yes, Kelly," said Hank with tears in his eyes. "I think we're going home."

It was a U.S. Coast Guard helicopter. A rescue diver jumped out of the airship into the ocean. He helped each of them climb into a basket, which was hoisted up on a cable. They were immediately wrapped in blankets. They were headed home.

Kelly took one last look at the ocean below. A large pod of dolphins suddenly came into view. As the helicopter flew away, Kelly thought she saw two dolphins jump high into the air and one did a somersault. She wondered if it had a scar running down its head.

"Thank you," she whispered, "again."

The rescue diver on board yelled to Hank over the roar of the rotating blades.

"Are you Hank Tenamaker?"

"Yeah, I am," responded Hank, very surprised. "How'd you know that?"

"The EPIRB, the Emergency Position Indicator Radio Beacon, from the plane you rented. It began signaling a couple of hours ago. No one could believe it since that plane's been missing for over a year."

"It's a long story," said Hank, thankful he had put it in the boat before they left the island. The EPIRB was designed to go on automatically when submerged underwater and must have been activated when the boat flipped over.

"And who are you?" shouted the diver to Kelly.

"Kelly Wickmer," she answered proudly.

The man looked at her as if he'd seen a ghost and said something into the microphone on his headset.

"Well, there are going to be some mighty happy people to see the both of you back on shore," said the Coast Guard diver, shaking his head and winking at Kelly. "Stranger things have happened, I guess. You know we are in the Bermuda Triangle."

Epilogue

When Mr. and Mrs. Wickmer got the news, they couldn't believe what they were hearing. It had been weeks since their daughter had disappeared at sea and they had lost all hope. They were gloriously happy, overjoyed, and Thomas, who had been in a severe depression ever since the accident, smiled for the first time since. They immediately arranged to travel to Miami, Florida, to be reunited with their daughter.

After a quick checkup at a nearby hospital and an overwhelming number of questions from the Coast Guard, the Navy, and lots and lots of reporters, both Hank and Kelly were resting comfortably in a fancy hotel on Miami Beach. Hank's two older sons, their families, and even his ex-wife were on their way to Miami from Colorado.

Kelly's parents were due to arrive at the hotel any moment. She was in the bathroom in her hotel room looking in the mirror. She had on the two-piece blue-and-white wrap decorated with dolphins that she had been wearing when they left the island. It had been washed and dried. She was the same girl as before, but she was also very different. Her hair was light blond with streaks of white framing her face. She was tan and from weeks of eating lots of fish, fruit, and vegetables combined with swimming and running around the island, she had grown very fit and now looked quite athletic. But it was the inside of Kelly that had changed even more.

She felt confident, brave, adventurous, and happy with who she was. And she certainly wasn't average anymore, but the funny thing was that it didn't matter. She now realized that it wasn't what you looked like or how you compared with anyone else. It didn't matter if you were shy or outgoing or if you had webbed hands or feet, shiny skin, or cloudy eyes. What really mattered was how you felt about yourself and how you treated other people—who you were on the inside. She also realized that the change had come from within herself, not from others noticing her or treating her differently.

Then Kelly thought of Dolphin Island, its residents, and the coral reef surrounding it. She thought of all the adventures she'd had, with the dolphins, with the rays, in the cave and waterfall pool, cruising down River Run, and with the shark. She couldn't wait to see her family, but she would miss the friends she had made on the island, especially Jack and Paroe. She wished she could see them again, wondering if Paroe really could talk to animals and if Jack would ever really catch the crab outside his house. Kelly would also miss the creatures of the sea she had gotten to know, particularly the dolphin, Slash, who had saved her twice. She wondered why he had rescued her. She was sad that in all likelihood she would never have a chance to find out or even see the dolphin again. Kelly also wondered if she would ever again dive beneath the bright blue waters of a coral reef, swim among its colorful inhabitants, or fly through the sea beside a dolphin.

She and Hank had agreed not to say very much, except to their families, other than that they were both stranded on a small tropical island. They wanted to protect Dolphin Island and weren't sure if anyone would believe them even if they did tell the whole truth. Kelly wondered if there was another passage to the island. She didn't think the twisting way the dolphins had led them through the reef was the same way she had been brought to the island. She wished that one day she could find her way back to Dolphin Island and once again see her friends—on land and in the sea.

There was a knock at the door and Kelly ran to open it. There stood her parents and her brother. For a moment they all remained motionless, just staring at one another. Then, in a rush of tears and laughter, they ran together into a great huddle.

Caroline Wickmer stepped back and looked her daughter over from head to toe, making sure she was real. She pinched her own arm to confirm that it wasn't a dream. It was real, and it was really Kelly. Her brother, Thomas, wiped tears from his eyes and gave Kelly an embrace so tight she could barely breathe.

After many, many hugs and tears of joy, the family sat down in the hotel suite. They couldn't stop smiling. Kelly sat close, next to her mother.

"We love you so much and are so thankful that you're home," said her mother.

"Me too," said Kelly happily, squeezing her mother tightly.

James Wickmer looked his daughter over carefully. What he noticed most was that her beautiful green eyes now absolutely sparkled with excitement. She exuded a great self-confidence. And he asked the one question they were all dying to know the answer to.

"So what really happened out there?"

Kelly smiled knowingly.

"Next vacation, can we go somewhere to see dolphins? And I've been thinking…I'd really like to learn to scuba dive."

The End

The Real Deal

Although this book is a fictional tale, much of it is based on real science. Here are just a few of the fun facts that were incorporated into the story.

- Many of the ocean's creatures produce light, a phenomenon known as bioluminescence. Most often it is seen at night as sparkling or pinpoint flashes of light when water motion disrupts the sea's small drifting plants, called phytoplankton. Jellyfish and other animals can also create glowing blue-green flashes of light.

- The black spiny sea urchin, *Diadema,* really does have spines tipped with poison, and the tips do often get stuck in people's skin...and yes, the acidity of urine will help to dissolve the calcium carbonate of the spines.

- Stingrays do not bite, but they do have a sharp barb on their tail that, when stepped on, can cause a painful injury. If stingrays are in the area, it is best to do the "stingray shuffle," dragging your feet in the sand to scare them off.

- A chemical from a coral that lives in very shallow water on the reef has been used to make sunscreen.

- Dolphins do use sound to create a picture of their surroundings—a technique known as echolocation—but it remains poorly understood.

- At night on the reef, some parrotfish do sleep in holes and spin a web of toxic mucus around themselves for protection from predators.

- Genips are a real fruit that grows on trees in tropical habitats.
- Volcanic ash can make soil very fertile for growing crops.
- Beachrock does form square blocks that can look like a road. In fact, a section of beachrock submerged in the Bahamas was once thought to be a road to the lost city of Atlantis.
- There are some tropical islands where salt is mined from the ocean by evaporation on wide sand flats.
- In the Bahamas there are caves with creamy tan, smooth stalactites and stalagmites that formed when sea level was lower.
- In the Florida Keys and a few other places, there are fossil coral reefs now sitting above sea level. Some have been mined for construction. You can see fossil coral skeletons in the ground and even in the walls of some of the hotels in the Florida Keys.
- Many of our medicines are derived from plants. The ocean is now becoming an important frontier for the discovery of new medicines because many of the sea's creatures use chemicals to defend themselves from predators.
- Mangroves are nurseries for young fish, and they do either exclude salt from their roots or excrete it on their leaves.
- Wetlands play an important role in filtering out pollution from water that flows off the land and into the ocean.
- In the Galapagos Islands there are marine iguanas that eat algae and get rid of salt by sneezing it out.
- People are developing new and improved ways to farm fish that do not hurt the environment and can help to feed the world's growing population.
- Sharks are not vicious people-eaters, as they are so often portrayed, but are graceful, sleek predators that play a critical role in the ocean ecosystem. Most shark incidents are cases of mistaken identity, and humans are usually spit out as an unworthy meal. Sharks have more

to fear from humans than vice versa, and many shark populations have been dramatically reduced due to overfishing.

- Many of the creatures described in this book, from sharks to trigger-fish to sea urchins and iguanas, are threatened by human activities; conservation is essential to preserving the ocean and its animals for the future.

To learn more about the ocean and opportunities to get involved, check out the following Web sites:

Education & Information
www.vims.edu/bridge
www.jasonproject.org
www.sea.edu
www.noaa.education.gov
www.oceanexplorer.noaa.gov
www.sanctuaries.noaa.gov/education/
www.seacamp.org
www.mrdf.org/mlhome.htm

Other Organizations
www.nsgo.seagrant.org
www.coastalamerica.gov
www.reef.org
www.coreocean.org
www.onr.navy.mil/focus/
www.blueoceaninstitute.org
www.earthecho.org
www.oceanconservancy.org
www.oceanfutures.org
www.oceansforyouth.org
www.fknms.nos.noaa.gov

Aquariums etc
www.flaquarium.org
www.mbayaq.org
www.sheddaquarium.org
www.aqua.org
www.mote.org
www.neaq.org
www.seaworld.org
www.discoverycove.com
www.auduboninstitute.org/aoa/
www.mysticaquarium.org
waquarium.otted.hawaii.edu
www.seattleaquarium.org
www.aquariumofpacific.org

Universities and Institutions
www.rsmas.miami.edu
www.whoi.edu
www.hboi.edu
www.sio.ucsd.edu
www.uncw.edu/aquarius
www.marine.usf.edu

Many of the adventures in this book are based on the real-life experiences of the author. To contact or learn more about her, go to www.earth2ocean.net.

To learn more about the illustrator, go to www.kalonbaquero.com.

A percentage of the profits from sales of this book will go toward marine education.

About the Author

Dr. Ellen Prager is a marine scientist and author of popular science and children's books. Many of the adventures in this book are based on her own experiences. She has lived in St. Croix and the Bahamas, and traveled to places such as the Galapagos Islands and Papua New Guinea. Dr. Prager is an experienced scuba diver and has lived underwater in an undersea research station for weeks at a time. She is a frequently requested public speaker and often appears as an expert on television. To learn more, visit her website: www.earth2ocean.net.

978-0-595-35791-8
0-595-35791-1

Printed in the United States
47669LVS00005B/217-270

9 780595 357918